A MINOR DETOUR

The Second In A Modern Trilogy

A MINOR DETOUR

L.B. LEWIS

A MINOR DETOUR

Copyedited by Sadye Scott-Hainchek
Cover by Elizabeth Griffin

ISBN 978-0-9978928-3-3 (Paperback)
ISBN 978-0-9978928-2-6 (E-Book)

http://www.lblewis.com

CONTENTS

Chapter 1
The Albatross

"Who is your new boyfriend, Sierra? Lexie told us that you were seeing someone over there," my Mom asked.

"Oh, haha. Yeah, I'm seeing someone. He's great!" I said, wondering how much Lexie had told Mom, even though I'd told her not to say anything. Changing the subject, I asked, "How are you doing? Getting the house ready for Lexie's party?"

"I'm fine. The house is a disaster with your father trying to fix everything and nothing at the same time. He's outside now doing something...God knows what." She let out a sigh, then continued, "But, Sierra Wellington, sometimes you are so naïve. You have to watch out because he probably is just using you to come to the U.S. And, now, all over the news, these people like him are being deported. Does he even speak English? Oh, your father just walked in. Hon, Sierra's on Skype talking about her new boyfriend, some foreigner who doesn't speak English," my Mom said and moved out of the way to let my Dad take over the conversation.

"Hi, Dad. Mom, of course he speaks English," I shyly said, wondering why she was acting like this. In my opinion, she couldn't be picky what language he spoke if he was going to take the albatross off her hands.

"Hi, Sierra. What kind of job does this guy

have? You can tell a lot about a man by the kind of work he does," said my Dad, looking seriously pissed as he narrowed his eyes into the camera.

"He's working on a few projects right now," I replied, hoping that this answer would suffice.

Mom came back into focus as she pushed my Dad out of the way, "Is he coming with you so we can meet him? You know your aunt Pattie is good at knowing if someone is a liar or not. She's coming to the party, and she's going to make her famous cannolis! Everyone is so happy for Lexie. You know, we haven't had a big party like this since, I think, Lexie's first Communion." She trailed off down memory lane.

"That was a long time ago," I said, cutting the nostalgic trip short. "I'm looking at flights now and will let you know what I end up doing. What date is the party again?" I asked, looking at my computer's calendar.

"August 19. You know, just bring this new boyfriend of yours. We'll pay for your tickets. When I was dating your father, my mother didn't like him either. But we've been together almost thirty years! And if someone is finally willing to take care of you, he can't be that bad," she said, laughing.

"Cute, Mom. Gotta go," I said, not laughing, ending the Skype call immediately.

I closed my laptop, poured a glass of rosé, put one ice cube in, and went out on the back patio to get some air. I knew I had to go home for this party or my ass was going to be grass. This party for Lexie was all consuming. I wasn't sure why everyone was making such a big deal about her graduating. The party that we'd had for my business school graduation was small and included a cake from Dairy Queen in the basement apartment in D.C. My self-consciousness jumped to the conclusion that maybe my parents were overcompensating for my choices to the tune of "See, everyone, we raised one normal daughter!"

After staying in Europe illegally for almost four months, I was ready to get on a plane and go back, unemployed but not alone.

Chapter 2
Hipsters (Seven Months Earlier)

Sitting at the gate of San Francisco International Airport, waiting for the fog to clear, I wondered whether I should text anyone to tell them I was leaving. I scrolled through the saved names on my phone, trying to remember their faces.

For the record, even if I had gotten a job in San Francisco, I would not have stayed. The weather was nice sometimes, and there were a lot of jobs. But the people were so strange there. Everyone was too similar: They dressed the same in hipster, tight-pant fashion; talked the same, saying "amazing" all the time; and had the same digital prosthetic soul in the form of a smartphone. *And they can all be the same together*, I told myself as I began to delete every 415 number.

When I was at the end of the alphabet in my contact list, I heard, "Do you know when we're going to get on the plane? I've got to get to Madrid by tonight for my gig."

As he waited for my answer, I sized him up in a few seconds: the same as all dudes in San Francisco. Entitled, bearded hipster tech worker making gobs of money wearing sperm-count-lowering skinny jeans and a wannabe lumberjack fitted plaid flannel shirt with a zip-up hoodie sweatshirt. He probably wore a skirt once a year at Burning Man, had a box of costumes and wigs under his bed, experimented with OneTaste, and tried an orgy courtesy of Craigslist.

By the looks of his new iPhone, gigantic headphones, leather luggage, and designer clothes, he was the target demographic to buy a unit in the new building that would replace my SRO. I had a pang of resentful animosity for his assumed lack of financial chaos and thought about Bev trying to find a new home so more of his kind could live comfortably in San Francisco. I had no sympathy for him if he would miss some gig in Madrid. I did have sympathy for my old neighbors, especially Bev.

"No, sorry," I spat out and looked down in a victimized way for both myself and Bev. *I hope I don't sit next to you nor see one of your kind after I leave San Francisco* was the secondary part that I said only to myself.

I had time to kill due to the fog delay, and I decided to write Bev a postcard since she didn't have a computer or email address. In less than two months from today, she had to find a new place to live, and I was worried about her. We'd gotten to be friends the past few weeks, and she always gave me her honest opinion peppered with stories about when she was my age. I decided to go buy a postcard at the airport gift shop and write her a quick note before her address changed.

While I was looking for the perfect card for

Bev, I heard a man's voice I recognized but couldn't figure out where I knew it from. I casually hid behind the rotating card rack, pretending to be looking, but really tuning in to what the man was saying.

"I can't wait until we get to Beijing and have some time alone," said a woman carrying a large Chanel travel bag.

"Babe, I've got to work. I don't think your uncle is going to be happy with me because there's no way we can speed up getting all those tenants out in two months," said the voice I knew.

"He'll just give you more money to take care of it. Just think of this: The sooner you do that, the faster our penthouse can be built. Just kick those sorry people out on the street. It's probably better than that dump anyway." Then she laughed.

The more I wanted to stare, the less I knew I should. I was frozen like a statue with a postcard in my hand; only my eyes followed the couple to the cash register. I could now clearly see the man: It was Steve, my former boss from the San Francisco office of Brown and White. He was the one who'd had me do all that research on SROs in San Francisco and used my work to broker the deal with the Chinese investor who, by the looks of things right now, was related to this Asian woman he was traveling with.

I assumed that either he had met this woman before or after the first deal, and that she was what facilitated the second luxury development that was fast-tracked by the city of San Francisco. What also was unsettling to me was that Brown and White had played a role in my eviction and also fired me for being passionless. Well, Steve and this woman sure were passionate in a capitalistic way: brimming with desire for their new penthouse, which caused all the people in the SRO to be evicted.

Engaged in the moment and unaware of the ex-employee staring from behind the postcard rack, they went out of the store without looking back. It was now safe for me to buy the postcard and stamp, then sit down to write to Bev.

Hi Bev,

How are you? My flight is delayed, and I thought I'd write you. I really hope you will find a nice new home soon. Thank you again for your support. I don't know what Madrid will be like but I'm positive it will be better than San Francisco. And I have a job, so that is a good thing! This year is going to be awesome! Write me at my parents' address in Detroit, and I'll write you back when I get my address in Madrid.

Take care,

Sierra

Chapter 3
Family Planet

After mailing the postcard, I walked back to my gate. First-class high rollers, people needing assistance, a handful of families, and then the rest of us economy passengers anxiously boarded. Of course, the trendy hipster was in the first-class group. The boarding process seemed laborious after waiting through a delay of two hours, which resulted in relative silence.

When I entered the plane, there were still many empty seats in the economy section. I found my aisle seat in a row of three that was already occupied by a little girl and her mother. Taking a look behind our row, I saw the grandmother and the older sister counterpart to the mom and little sister. Then, an older, unrelated woman took the seat directly behind me.

"Are you traveling alone?" asked the mother, glaring at me as I stuffed my backpack under the seat.

"Yes, I'm alone," I responded suspiciously.

"Are you alone? Are you traveling by yourself?" repeated the mother, this time to the older woman behind me.

"I don't understand why you are asking me this," replied the woman.

"I didn't want anyone to sit near my family. They assured me I would have the two rows for my girls. I don't know why they put single people here when I asked them not to."

This woman obviously had major control issues. Being on family planet for ten hours to London would be too much for me to handle. I didn't like to be treated with such suspicion, like I was going to kidnap her kids or was a carrier for some disease I didn't even know I had. I got up to talk to the flight attendant to ask whether I could move away from the weirdos who'd just busted out an eight-piece bucket of KFC. As I approached the flight attendant, the mother snuck up behind me.

"You see, she is alone, and they put her next to my family. She needs to move because I don't want anyone sitting near us," the mother said without even looking at me, as if I weren't human.

"I'd like to change seats after takeoff. Is that possible?" I asked in a calm way. I made eye contact with the flight attendant to show how serious I was about not letting this situation last the duration of an international flight.

"We don't have a full flight, so you can change after we are in the air," the flight attendant said with a smile. "We are preparing for takeoff, and I'll need you both to go back to your seats now."

The ding of the bell was heard, and that was our cue to go back to our original seats. By the time we got to our row, more fried chicken had been eaten, and I saw that the other single traveler had already moved.

"Why are you going to Madrid by yourself? Do you have a Spanish husband waiting for you, too?" the mother asked me, then glanced down at my hands to look for a ring.

"I got a job in Madrid, and I hope I find a boyfriend there," I said with a slight smile, thinking this woman is crazy.

"Well, my girls' father is Spanish, and we're going for two months to find our new home. We can't afford the San Francisco Bay Area anymore. And we want to live in a safer place that has less crime, street people, and marijuana. The Bay Area is only good if you work in technology."

"Oh, I see. Do your girls speak Spanish?"

"Of course. We sent them to a bilingual school in Berkeley until we decided to home-school them. In Madrid, you know, it's more family oriented, more conservative than the Bay Area, so they will go to the private school that my husband attended. They can even come home for lunch every day. Honestly, I think it's going to be hard for you because you are by yourself now, but once you find a Spanish boyfriend, you'll fit in better."

"OK," I said, with no other words coming to mind after that last sentence. So apparently single people didn't fit in on a plane *or* in Madrid. This interaction added to what little I already knew about

Spain. I knew that they spoke Spanish, conquered Latin America, and liked soccer. Just now, I'd learned that the culture may be hostile towards single woman. This was a reminder that I had to read my guidebook after I changed seats to learn more about Spanish culture. Hopefully there was a section on Spanish men because I needed to understand whether Cristian was interested in dating me.

"Is there any fried chicken left, Martina?" asked the mother of her younger daughter.

"One piece for you, Mom."

"Thank you, sweetie."

The plane began its ascent with the aroma of fried chicken lingering in the cabin. I changed seats quickly when the "Fasten Seatbelt" sign was turned off to claim a middle row of three seats for my family: me, myself, and I. I hoped the delay in San Francisco would not make me miss my connection to Madrid. I couldn't miss that because Cristian would be waiting for me.

Chapter 4
Preparing for Possibilities

I had ten hours to think of what the next three months would hold for me. My heart was open to possibilities, but I still needed to prepare for everything else. I'd bought a new notebook before I left to make sure I was organized with my "Things to Do" list on the first page.

First, I was going to meet Cristian at the Ibiza metro stop. Not sure whether this was where the apartment was, I was hoping that Cristian would pick me up in his black Mercedes convertible or some other expensive car with leather seats that had built-in heaters to keep my bottom toasty. We wouldn't go straight to the apartment; instead I'd suggest that we go out to eat, and he would take me to the best restaurant in Madrid where he would know everyone there and introduce me as his American girlfriend who was finally in Spain. I'd be thrilled to toast with the vintage champagne that cost more than my monthly rent in Houston. Even though I didn't like to drink after a long flight, I'd make an exception this one time. It would be a special occasion, after all. And this restaurant would be way too fancy to use ParaLlevar—that was the true sign of moving up the food chain. Cristian created ParaLlevar for the working-class, sharing-economy, and app-addict types, but wouldn't use it himself. By a stroke of much-deserved luck, I would now be free from the confines of the drudgery of job searching, networking, and other mundane white-collar tasks to take on my new role as the Mrs. to the Mr. of a Spanish dynasty. I'd probably have to start organizing next year's charity gift-giving event right away and look into getting Botox for the premature wrinkles I was getting.

Back to reality. Second, there was also a section that I made in my notebook with dates of my loan and credit card payments, which I had to at least try to keep on making while I was there—until Cristian offered to pay off my loans. I hadn't made my January payments yet because I wasn't sure how I was going to get paid for this job. Since I didn't have a Spanish bank account, I was going to ask for my salary to be wired to my U.S. bank account. I had some calculations written here about the budget I had to keep, but in actuality, I had no idea how much it was going to cost me to live in Madrid or if things didn't go well with Cristian.

Related to making my loan payments, the next item was drafting a backup plan. This was something I had no previous experience in, but I had to plan to set aside a little money in case I had an emergency or needed to fly back to the U.S. These savings would be the refunded SRO security deposit that I was still waiting to receive.

I put the notebook in the back pocket of the seat in front of me, and I fell asleep. The next thing

I knew, there was a disgusting-looking breakfast waiting for me on the neighboring tray table. The discolored fruit salad with the red cherry bleeding on the green honeydew did not look like food at all. I was still so tired and groggy, my heavy head gravitated to my tray table to leave my breakfast uneaten.

My head hit my notebook sticking out of the seat pocket on the way down. I wanted to go back to sleep, but my brain was now awake and asking questions. What was I about to do? Was I in love with Cristian? I admitted to myself that I didn't really know what love was, beyond a four-letter word that people sometimes say at the end of an email or card. From time to time, when someone texted "luv u," I wondered whether it was a command to love oneself or a sincere abbreviated form of "I love you." And then when your parents or grandparents said it while you were having a hard time or they were drunk, it seemed like a momentary way to make someone feel better, and that someone is not always the recipient. Romantic love, for me as an adult and not a college student, was an alien concept just like having a career and job I felt good about.

But I was going to try both and add to my professional and dating resumes in a new city, Madrid. I sat back up and grabbed my guidebook. Paging through it for the first time, I admired the elegant buildings and famous artwork by Picasso and Velázquez featured in its color photographs—as

well as Spanish food. The actual restaurant descrip-
tions were appetizing, too, but even the ones marked
with one euro seemed too expensive for my budget.
A couple of maps that were included seemed decent.
Then, coming to the end of the book, I searched the
index for the "Dating a Spaniard" section only to
discover that it wasn't that type of guidebook.

With a sigh, I looked at the calendar on my
cellphone and put my head back on the tray table.
I had one week to acclimate, mainly to get over jet
lag, before I needed to go to the office and begin
working. Then, I would have until April 15, when
my ninety days would be up and I would have to
return to the U.S., just in time to pay my taxes.
There had been no contract for me to sign with
Cristian about the duration and conclusion of my
three months in Madrid. There was also no return
ticket for me either.

I sat up after hearing a child start crying. This
flight was never going to end. I still had to process
the earlier offensive incident of the seat assignment
next to that family. I wondered whether what that
mother told me about being single in Madrid was
true. But, instead of telling me how hard it was
going to be for me in Madrid, why hadn't I cut that
mother off and asked her about how hard it was to
push two babies out?

I told myself that I must ask more questions
because no one was sharing with me how difficult
it was to pay off loans and be a working woman, let

alone find a husband or to give birth. No little girl dreams of loans, dating apps, and being a spinster. There was no Disney movie like that, at least not yet.

Chapter 5
Spare Apartment

By some miracle, my flight from London to Madrid was also delayed. I made it to the gate with a half hour to spare and saw the family again. This time they were eating fish and chips. We all boarded the plane and I cringed to think about what was going to happen but at least this time they had their own rows.

The flight went by quickly and, as the plane approached Madrid, the sun was shining brightly across the barren winter landscape. Even though it was sunny, the temperature on the in-flight entertainment system said eight degrees Celsius or forty-six degrees Fahrenheit. I had to learn how to convert to Celsius at some point, but right now I wanted to get my purple puffer winter coat out as soon as I picked up my bags.

My heartbeat was gradually getting faster as I got my bags, put on my coat, and walked to the metro. The train car was brightly lit and very clean. People were orderly about taking a seat or standing. There was some Spanish chatter that sounded like an unintelligible murmur to me. I sat down near the door with my two suitcases and decided to look at the metro map in the guidebook. It seemed weird to look at a book instead of my phone, but until I got my SIM card, I would have to rely on this book. I anxiously wondered whether there were any unscrupulous people waiting to prey on clueless Americans with guidebooks and suitcases.

The plan was that Cristian would be waiting outside the Ibiza metro exit at 2:00 PM, or so he'd said in his last email to me. Even with the flight delays, I was on time. Expecting that he wouldn't be there because he was busy doing more important things at ParaLlevar, I decided to invent more scenarios to feed my anxiety like I would either have to wait for him or try to find a place with WiFi to call him from Skype using my computer.

I was too focused on my anxiety and suitcases to immediately notice that he was waiting for me, just as he'd said in the email. He was standing only a few feet away from the metro exit with an open long black overcoat to show his white dress shirt and well-fitting dark gray wool suit.

"*Bienvenida*, Sierra!" he said while giving me the customary greeting of two kisses.

"¡*Hola!* I made it!" I awkwardly said, avoiding eye contact. My leftover anxiety of expecting that he wasn't going to be there was now transferred to a feeling of being embarrassed at the way I looked. *I could have spruced myself up at the airport, or at least brushed my hair*, I thought as I nervously adjusted my purple puffer jacket. He looked more handsome than I remembered, with his genuine smile and dapper coat.

"Let me take you to the apartment now. It's just

a five-minute walk from here. Then, I have to go back to the office. We have a lot of work to do," he said, taking my two suitcases in his strong hands as if they were nothing to him.

I followed a few steps behind. He seemed preoccupied with trying to push the suitcases and wasn't talking. After five minutes of walking, I realized that he probably wasn't going to talk at all. Maybe he didn't want to speak in English to attract attention. My focus was now on the stores and restaurants that we were passing. The restaurants looked pretty nice, and there were some small shops for women, shoes, and household items. The street looked a lot cleaner than San Francisco, with no trash or feces in sight, and the neighborhood seemed to be pretty safe, with a good number of normal-looking people around and no noticeable homeless people or marijuana dealers.

"Here we are. Look, you put the code 1226#, and then you use this fob to get into the lobby. I'll put your suitcases in the elevator, and you can ride with them to the fourth floor. I'll take the stairs."

"OK, thank you," I said as the doors closed on the smallest elevator I'd ever seen. I had to rest my elbow on my vertically stacked suitcases.

When the elevator got to the fourth floor, the doors opened, and Cristian was already standing in front of the apartment door, smiling holding the keys.

"This is my little apartment. Sometimes I rent it out to students, but usually it's empty. The building has a cleaning lady that comes every week, and she takes care of the lobby. If you want, I'll have her clean your apartment, too. Just let me know. My family has owned this building for many years, so we have a good relationship with everyone here. And I trust you will not have any crazy parties, but if you do, invite me, please," he said, laughing. I laughed too, relieved that he seemed to be a different person here. We walked to the end of the hallway and he opened the door to the apartment.

"Thank you, Cristian. I'm really happy to be here," I said smiling and standing up straight, extending my chin so I looked more elegant despite my unkemptness. I wanted to flirt, but I didn't know how, and I also desperately needed a shower.

"Great. I hope you can help ParaLlevar and think this could be a good experience for all of us to learn from each other. I think you know how to use everything in this apartment. There are no surprises here except the couch has a bed," he said, as he removed one of the cushions.

"I have to go, Sierra. If you get a bill or any other thing in the mail for me, just tell me and then put it in the drawer here. I pay them all online anyway. Call me on the number in the email I sent you last week if you need anything, and I'll see you on Monday," he said as he touched my right shoulder and kissed both cheeks again.

"Thank you very much, Cristian. See you next Monday," I said as I followed him to the door.

While I understood he was in a hurry and also I was not looking or feeling my best after being on a transatlantic flight, I had at least wanted him to invite me for lunch or tell me where to go in the neighborhood to get something to eat. Maybe he would fill me in the next time I saw him, I told myself to ease my disappointment.

Looking around with my back against the door, I had a good view of the apartment. It was very small, only about two hundred square feet in total. Definitely the smallest apartment I'd ever lived in. The walls were white and completely bare. There was just enough space for the pullout sofa, a bookcase with nothing in it, and a double bed. The double bed was almost too large for the space with only a few inches on the left side of the bed to access the closet. I opened the closet's sliding door to find a small area for hanging clothes and three drawers on one side and a few shelves with towels and sheets on the other side. Picturing my clothes and suitcases fitting in, I slid the door back to close it.

Then I took a walk into the kitchen. The kitchen had a small fridge, an electric range with two burners, a toaster, and a washing machine. *Why would a washing machine be in the kitchen?*

I thought. The best reason I could think of was that if you spilled something on yourself, you could just take it off while preparing your dinner and wash it right away so that the stain would not set in. Genius. I looked out the window of the kitchen to see, straight ahead and down to the right, the roof of a smaller building that probably was a store.

The best part of the whole apartment was in the bathroom. While the round corner shower was a bit strange, the electric towel warmer was phenomenal. I'd only ever seen these in the *SkyMall* magazine and never would've believed that someone had actually bought one for a little apartment like this. I'd always thought they were a luxury bathroom accessory for people who had money—and towels—to burn. I couldn't wait to try it.

Walking to the bed, I lay down on my back with my feet still on the ground. This was really happening! My new life in Madrid in a nice apartment. Everything was on track, at least for the next three months. I couldn't believe Cristian owned this whole building and I wouldn't have to pay rent. He must be super rich, a lot richer than I'd imagined.

Chapter 6
Desk with a View

My secret fantasy of a passionate love affair starting the second I got to Madrid continued to exist only in my head. I vacillated between thinking of my responsibility to pay off my loans with romantic daydreams of Cristian being my boyfriend. It would be so much fun to go on weekend getaways to his country home or to get dressed up to go to fancy four-course dinner parties.

But during my first week, I only saw Cristian once, when I'd first arrived, and he didn't even recommend anywhere to eat. But he *had* said that he had to go back to the office, and maybe he'd also been tired then. Things might be different once I started working and got to see him every day.

The first day of work arrived, and I wasn't sure what to wear. It was strange because I hadn't seen one hipster. Everyone seemed well dressed with nicely tailored clothes, scarves, hats, and coats on the streets of Madrid, even kids. And there seemed to be a lot of them around.

There were so many traditional families and strollers that I now realized what the woman on the plane had meant. Husband, wife, stroller, with or without a side kid, grandparent optional. Family values and family time seemed to be very important. Clothes that were clean, pressed, and well-fitting also seemed important. I wondered what people would wear at ParaLlevar.

Truthfully, I really wanted to look nice for Cristian, but I also had to make a good first impression on everyone else. I never wanted to repeat that moment when Pamela, my old mentor at Brown and White, had said I had to pay more attention to how I looked at the office. Furthermore, I couldn't forget to ask about my salary, so I had to wear something conservative, classy, and a little trendy, since it was still a startup.

I chose the dress I bought to interview with in San Francisco. I put the dress on the electric towel warmer during my shower so that both the steam from the shower and the electric heater could work out the wrinkles. Surprisingly, there were relatively few wrinkles left after my shower and was thrilled that the towel warmer proved itself to be multi-purpose.

I decided to walk to the office which was about a forty-minute walk from the studio. I didn't want to take the bus and make a fool of myself in Spanish. Besides, I had to keep on saving money where I could and see as much of Madrid as possible.

While walking there, I noticed that the neighborhoods were changing, and the closer I got to the office, the more upscale it seemed to be, judging by the stores El Corte Inglés, Hoss Intropia, and Adolfo Dominguez. Since I'd left early to avoid having to rush, I now had extra time and slowed down to do some window shopping. The fashionable styles looked refined and untouchable, just like the prices. The perfectly coordinated ensembles of dress, scarf, jacket, belt, bracelet, and handbag made me wonder whether I could pull off this look with everything I brought to Madrid. I did want to look good, but these stores would break the bank for me. I would stick to the low-cost options of Zara and Mango, which wasn't that awful; I liked their clothes.

Glancing at the time, I ended my window shopping and walked briskly to the address that Cristian gave me for ParaLlevar. In about ten minutes, I was standing in front of an eight-story gray stone building and, upon entering, was relieved to see ParaLlevar listed on the directory. The building was pretty nice, almost too nice for a startup, and not like the kind that I'd seen in San Francisco. This *was* Europe, after all, and maybe ParaLlevar was part of something larger. I still didn't know a lot about Cristian and had more than a few blanks to fill in, both on his personal and professional life.

"*Buenos días*, Sierra. Welcome to ParaLlevar!" Cristian greeted me with the standard two kisses as I entered the office space.

"Hi, Cristian," I said as my cheek touched his and my nose inhaled his clean-smelling aftershave. The scent lingered in my mind as I pictured him putting it on this morning in front of the mirror in his plush white bathrobe.

"How are you? Everything OK in the apartment?"

"Yes, thank you. It's perfect," I said, still daydreaming about his morning bathroom rituals.

"I'm happy to hear that. We just got your new desk ready on this side of the office. My other company is over here. ParaLlevar is just one part of what I do," he said, then looked behind him to motion another man to come over. "Alex, please meet Sierra."

"Hi, Sierra. I'm Alex. It's a pleasure," he said as he held his hand out to shake mine. His hand was all bone like his body. His face showed he was about my age and had a classic Greek nose and bushy eyebrows. He had thick, gorgeous, straight brown hair to his shoulders that would make any woman jealous.

"Hi, Alex. Nice to meet you. What do you do at ParaLlevar?" I kept on staring at his hair, wondering whether he used a blow-dryer in the morning to get it so perfectly straight. He definitely was in touch with his feminine side.

"I'm the project manager. There are only three of us here, myself, Alex and Christian, so we all do a little of everything. Now you will be number four, just like a family," he said, chuckling.

"OK, can't wait!"

"Sierra, we'll all have a meeting tomorrow to talk about our goals and responsibilities for the next few months. Today, I'd like you to get settled in at your new desk and find a list of ten expat websites. Sites in English for the expat residents of Madrid: Americans, Brits, Canadians, Australians. You get the picture."

"Yes, I can do that. Where should I sit?"

"I'll show you the way," Alex said as he started walking.

"Thanks, Cristian."

"Thank you, Sierra. We're happy to have you here."

I caught up with Alex, who was now walking toward the corner of the floor. I was so surprised that my desk was near the window, in a corner. Upon further inspection, this desk had real drawers, not a rolling set of temporary file drawers. There was also a phone, a blue notebook, and two pens near the phone. Looking out the window, I had a great view of a store across the street called Jardin de los Sueños. Any store called "Garden of Dreams" with a pink sign, pink door frame, and pink window display must be for little girls.

"This is your desk, Sierra, and your laptop is in here, and the passwords are there, too," said Alex.

"Wow, great. Thank you."

"Let me know if you need anything. I am sitting over there."

"Thank you, Alex."

I opened the drawer to find the laptop and saw a notebook with the name "Melinda" on it. I just put that aside and took out the laptop. A profile named Melinda also came up when I turned on the laptop, and I used the passwords I found in the drawer to log in. I wondered whether I would meet Melinda tomorrow during the meeting. It would be great to have a female co-worker. Working in an all-male environment was something business school hadn't prepared me to do and I already failed at it during my stint at Brown and White. Back to my task at hand, I got straight away at making the list and finished before it was time to go home.

Chapter 7
Ready or Not

I knew I liked Spanish fashion, but I had no idea where to start with Spanish food. I had made a couple of trips to the corner store near the apartment but had stuck with crackers, pasta, tuna, and canned vegetables.

On my way to and from the office, I passed a rather strange mall that looked like it had a super-market inside called Mercadona. I figured it might be decent because the tagline on the sign said "*supermercados de confianza*," which translated to being the trusted supermarket.

When I entered, the orderliness and cleanliness reassured me that it had that tagline for a reason. Quickly, I came to the conclusion that pizza love was universal as the huge pizza section loomed on the horizon of the first aisle. So many types of pizza: *atún y bacon, cuatro quesos, margarita, jamón y queso, jamón serrano, romana, barbacoa, carbonara, mediterránea,* and *pepperoni.*

They were all less than three euros. I did some comparison calculations in my head and wondered why this pizza was so cheap. But then I thought, *who cares?* I could definitely afford to eat a pizza-based diet at that price. I loaded my cart with one *barbacoa,* one *margarita,* one *jamón serrano* and one *pepperoni.*

In my guidebook, I'd read about the egg and

potato omelet they called a *tortilla española* that you can eat cold or warm. They had a whole bunch of those at Mercadona. Since I was too intimidated to go by myself to a restaurant where they probably didn't speak English that well, I thought I would buy a *tortilla española* here along with my pizza, California salad, hummus, *triángulos de maíz* (aka tortilla chips), and walnuts, which were called *nueces de California*. That made me wonder whether I maybe shouldn't trust this place because they were trying to be American by calling walnuts Californian nuts. But, I reasoned, imitation is the highest form of flattery and my stomach wouldn't know the difference.

Putting my soon-to-be purchases on the conveyor belt, I looked adoringly at my amazing Spanish food chugging along and wondered what it would taste like. I tried to imagine that moment when the melted cheese on the pizza met my lips. Then, the woman at the register barked something at me in guttural Spanish. She barked again louder with her well-developed lung capacity. Then, after all the food was slid across the scanner, she looked at me, and we stared at each other for a few seconds.

"Oh, um, um, *pago con cardeta, por favor, Señora*," I said with a smile and held up my American Express.

"*No es cardeta. Es tarjeta*," she snapped as she quickly grabbed my card, swiped it, and printed out a receipt in the time it took my smile to fade into oblivion.

Maybe she was having a bad day. Or maybe my Spanish mistake really pissed her off, and that was why she didn't even thank me for making a purchase. The customer service at Mercadona could be overlooked for those prices and if the pizza was good.

After walking home with my heavy grocery bags, I sat down for a moment and turned on my computer. I signed in to Skype to see whether any friends were online. My Mom was online, and I called her while getting up to unload the groceries and put my pizza in the microwave oven combo.

"Hi, Sierra! How are you doing in Madrid? What time is it for you?" my Mom said over Skype video as she sat at the kitchen table drinking her coffee, still in her bathrobe.

"Hi, Mom. Everything is fine. It's 8:00 here, and I just got back from grocery shopping after work."

"How's work? And how is that apartment? Show me on video!"

"Well, it's small, and now it's kinda dark in here, but maybe another time I'll show you during the daytime when it's much lighter. I like the office, and the people seem nice."

"Oh, OK. Is your apartment big enough for guests?"

"There's a sofa bed, but I'm not sure anyone is going to visit. You know, I'm only here three months because I just have the tourist visa. Then, if everything is working out well, Cristian will sponsor a work visa for me."

"Well, Lexie is going to call you soon. Mario is going back to Italy in April for Easter, and they thought they would visit Madrid because Mario has a lot of friends there and now you're there, too. Just thought I'd mention that. They both came here for Christmas, and we were talking about your new adventure. You know, we missed you this year!"

"Oh yeah? It would be fun to have Lexie visit, but I'm not sure I want both of them staying in my place. It's really small."

"Honey, I'm sure you'll love Mario. *Everyone* does. Did you get my email about your loan payment? Navient called here, and I wasn't sure what to say or what was going on. I know you don't have a lot of money, but you need to keep paying your loans off. If you don't..."

"Oh, you know it was just a courtesy call. Everything is on track. I think my pizza is burning. Talk to you soon. Have a good night."

I closed Skype so fast I didn't even hear my Mom say goodbye. I went to the Navient site and tried to log in, but I couldn't remember my password. I knew the call that my Mom was referring to was actually because I missed my monthly payment. In the chaos to pack and sort out my finances, I deliberately did not make the January payment because I wasn't sure I could afford to get to Madrid and wasn't sure how long I would have to wait until I got my first paycheck here.

Once my new password email had arrived, I logged in to see a message about what I already knew. I quickly made the payment and realized I only had $100 left in my savings account until I got paid, and I wasn't sure when that would be. I also didn't know how I would pay the minimum on my credit card balances and eat with $100. I was no longer getting unemployment checks, and I was still waiting for my deposit on my SRO to come through, too. I just hoped to survive the next few weeks.

Then I Googled my sister to see whether I could find a picture of her and Mario. She was still on Facebook, but I couldn't see any pictures of them together from my search. If she visited, that could be fun, but how could I have her and her new boyfriend in this small apartment? I wondered how annoying she would be with this new guy of hers. Her last boyfriend was comparable to a lost puppy, and she, not unlike the bossy mother on the plane with her rugrats, attempted once to cut up his steak at a restaurant because he was doing a poor job of it. I hoped her standards had been raised after that relationship as she and our family definitely deserved better.

But, as I was thinking about my sister's visit, I thought how I didn't want to be the third wheel. After the two bad experiences in Houston, I was not going to do online dating ever again, but I thought I could try speed dating. I searched for speed dating in Madrid, and surprisingly I found an event that was scheduled for Saturday of this week. I quickly registered using my credit card, in sharp contrast to what I had just talked to myself about. To invest in my personal life was the next-best thing one could do. My emotional needs trumped my budget, and if I started now, I might have someone to introduce my sister to, too.

Chapter 8
Templates

"Hi, Sierra. How's everything going? You look very nice today, by the way," Cristian said from behind his desk, when I entered his office for our first one-on-one meeting. "Please close the door."

I was confused as to how this one-on-one was going to progress. While I still found him attractive and wanted something more with him outside the office, which hadn't happened yet, inside the office it was hard to understand what my job was, and I was trying to think of a way to tell him this.

Every day during my first two weeks, my responsibilities had grown. First, I had to make the list of expat sites that Cristian wanted. Then, Alex told me that I would be in charge of the blog and I had to write three blog posts that week about being a tourist in Madrid, what ParaLlevar does, and where to eat the best tapas in Madrid. I had never written a blog post before, and I didn't even know much about Madrid. As for tapas, I knew they were food, like appetizers or something but I had never tried them.

Alex had also told me to do some keyword research and copy what Melinda had done. It was all in the shared drive, he said, and I could use the templates. I did my best to learn, copy, and improve to achieve the goal of growing ParaLlevar's customers. I didn't have any numbers to hit or aggressive targets; I was just supposed to focus on making outreach and writing messaging, which I felt would keep me busy for the coming weeks, in addition to a big press release I was supposed to be writing for the new app.

"Thanks, Cristian. Everything is going well. I found the files you mentioned on the computer and some blog posts Melinda wrote. Does she still work here?" I asked and looked at him for a moment, then nervously shifted my gaze to his desk to see picture frames that were facing him.

"We had to let her go back to the U.S. She was another American intern, like you," he said, smiling at me like the Cheshire Cat. If he had a tail, it would have been thumping.

"I think I'm too old to be your MBA intern, Cristian. And I wanted to ask: When will I be getting paid?" I countered in a defensive way, which may have been too bold, but it was necessary to set my boundaries. I was also upset that he called me an intern. He obviously sensed my emotions and looked away from me and at his computer, pretending to do something.

"Just submit your monthly invoice to me. We usually pay thirty days after we get an invoice."

"I'm sorry, I can't wait that long. Is it possible we can sign a contract with the pay dates outlined? I'd prefer weekly or biweekly." I was on fire and confused first by his aloofness and now by his reluctance to put anything in writing. I was afraid I would be taken advantage of again or, worse, let go again. I also was feeling stressed at the daily increase in my assigned tasks that I had no experience in doing.

"Things move a lot slower in Spain than in the U.S., but don't worry, Sierra. Draft your contract today and send me an invoice for this week. You are considered a freelancer for us, so send me your hourly rate. If you want, after work today, I'll stop by your apartment and drop off an envelope with cash in it since I know you can't get a bank account here," he said smiling, turning the situation around by using his leadership abilities to make everyone feel it was a win-win situation.

"Thank you. Sounds good. Next week, I'll meet with Alex to learn about the new features for the app release. I'm learning a lot about tech and startups here. Alex is really helping me because I still have a few questions. It's a lot different than the other jobs I've had before."

"Great, Sierra. Send me your invoice and contract and I'll come over to the apartment around 7:00. I have to leave the office today at 4:00, but I'll make it there around 7:00."

"Thank you, Cristian. I appreciate it."

I walked back to my desk a little disoriented by the meeting that had begun with a compliment and ended with the offer to be paid in cash. The contract and invoice were already prepared; I'd found one of each in the shared drive when I'd been looking for past press releases. I would just use these templates and add my billable hourly rate in dollars, then convert to euros. That was surprisingly easy, and I calculated an hourly rate based on my salary at Brown and White as an analyst.

After my invoice and contract were emailed to Cristian, I kept on working on a blog post about being an American in Madrid. It was strange that I did not see Cristian leave. I did see some other people in the office were leaving around 6:00, so I took that as my cue to go home, too.

While taking the metro home, I decided I would not change out of my work clothes, so as not to seem too rehearsed when Cristian arrived. I got home around 6:30 and immediately put my suitcases under the bed and closed the closet. The kitchen and bathroom were clean, and I sat on the sofa waiting until I heard the doorbell ring.

At 7:00 PM, there was a knock at the door, and through the peephole, I saw Cristian, who looked freshly showered and shaved. His black hair was gelled, combed back in a style I hadn't seen before. This new hairstyle highlighted his forehead, which looked out of proportion with the rest of his face due to his receding hairline. He had changed his clothes and was now wearing his black overcoat and a forest green wool scarf. There was an envelope in his right hand, and he was holding a bottle of red wine in his left hand.

"Hi, Cristian. Come in, please," I said, smiling, then realizing that it sounded stupid since it was his apartment.

He took a step forward and transferred the envelope to his left hand. Instead of touching my shoulder, his right hand went to my waist as he gave me two kisses.

"Hi, Sierra. How are you? You know we haven't had a chance to talk much since you got here. Is everything going OK? Are you feeling OK?" His eyes met mine and looked like he was sincerely interested in knowing how I was doing, which was more than any other boss had ever done.

"Yes, I was just worried about money. Thank you for coming over with this week's pay. It takes a load off my mind. I also think I am going to start taking a Spanish class soon. And I'm going to focus on meeting people here."

"Good, Sierra. I brought you your money here, and this wine is for you, too. If you want, we can open it now and do a toast to your new job!"

"OK, sounds good. I don't know where you keep the corkscrew here. Which drawer is it in? I'll get the glasses."

"I'll find it for you." As he opened a few drawers, I saw him grab the corkscrew and a receipt that had been in the drawer with the bills. He casually put the receipt in his pocket and then came over to the sofa. Our eyes met, and he gave a little smile. Then he took off his scarf and jacket and put them on the arm of the sofa before he sat down next to me. Once seated, he grabbed the corkscrew and opened the wine bottle to pour two glasses. I was having hallucinations that this was our place and we were a cohabitating couple having our nightly drink.

"To Sierra's Spanish adventure," he said as he held up his glass for the toast.

"Cheers," I said making concentrated eye contact with him for the third time this evening.

A few sips later and I was finished with the first glass. I hadn't had dinner yet, so I was feeling a little bit tipsy already. Cristian got up to go to the bathroom, and his coat fell off the couch armrest. A receipt had fallen out of his pocket and landed on the floor near me. When he closed the bathroom door, I looked at the receipt. It was from that store near the office, Jardin de los Sueños. The amount was for 250 euros. I picked up the coat and the receipt when he walked out of the bathroom.

"Oh, let me get that, Sierra," he said, taking the coat and the receipt and again putting the receipt in his pocket.

We both sat back on the sofa, and this time he put his right arm around me. I was surprised, but I had also been wondering when this was going to happen. His hand started stroking my shoulder, then

I turned to look at him. His lips met mine. He held them there for a few seconds, pulled away for a few seconds, and then did it again. This could have been appropriately described as lip contact, just like when I was learning CPR on the plastic dummy in my lifeguarding class. I followed his lead, also not making any muscle or tongue movements. Maybe, like the French, the Spanish had their own kiss named after them. I would check online after this cultural exchange was over.

His other hand took my hip, just like the moment not more than thirty minutes ago when he'd greeted me. I realized while he was attractive and had great lips, this CPR practice was strange. He finally sensed my lack of interest and moved to my neck, and then I felt like I was back playing with my childhood dog, Max. Cristian was licking my neck just like Max did. I could not keep it in any longer and exploded with a snort and a burst of nervous laughter.

Cristian stopped suddenly and looked at me. "Sierra, why are you laughing?"

"I think we better stop, Cristian. It was my first time to do a Spanish kiss, and I'm not sure if it's for me," I said, still smiling. Then, trying to cover up my uncomfortableness, I added, "And I need to eat dinner."

"OK, Sierra. I have to go to a birthday party anyways. I'll see you on Monday." And with that, he left the apartment and did not even give me the customary two kisses. His seduction template and repertoire of romance were not my style, and now I was mix of tipsy, culture shocked, and disappointed.

Chapter 9
Speed Dating

After last night's failed romantic episode, my feelings toward Cristian began to change. I'd known there was a chance of this happening from the moment I met him in San Francisco, and while we did have some chemistry, I was confused. I was a bit disgusted with myself and with him. Maybe the women he had dated in the past liked his idea of romance, but what was also strange to me was that he'd seemed to have planned the whole evening, down to looking for the corkscrew and then taking the receipt.

I looked online for "Spanish kiss" but got no results that explained what Cristian was attempting to do. I reasoned with myself that keeping my job and getting paid were more important to me than pursuing something romantic with my boss, with whom an experiment had yielded poor physical compatibility. It was a very smart move for me to have signed up for the speed-dating event tonight to get my mind off what was going on or the ramifications on Monday. I needed to get over whatever it was that was making me desperate.

I ran errands, did my laundry, and had time for a nap before the event. When I woke from my nap, I double-checked where the venue for the event was. The club was on Calle del Príncipe, Prince Street in English, which was hilarious and a good omen at the same time. The organizers had surely done this on purpose for the attendees to feel hopeful about meeting someone special, maybe even their long-lost-prince soul mate. It set the stage for romance.

When I got to the street, the street sign even had a picture of a Spanish prince. But the club was less than royal. It was actually kind of seedy with an '80s feel to it as the red lights accented the black, fake leather furniture. Even the bar was lit from behind with a red light, making it look more like December than February. But, reminding myself that I hadn't come for the décor—I came to meet men—I entered with fearless determination.

I walked toward the organizer, who had a clipboard and a roll of pink tickets, at the bar. He explained to me, in Spanish, that I would have many *citas rápidas* that would last seven minutes. I smiled and said I was an American who was learning Spanish. He smiled back at me, said that was good because not many people spoke English, and handed me a pink drink ticket.

After I got a *calimocho* with my ticket, I walked to the back of the club where there was a group of women waiting for the event to begin. I went up to a dark-haired, petite woman who was wearing a shirt that said "Life is Beautiful." *Great*, I thought, *she must speak some English*. We started chatting in

Spanish and then quickly changed to English when I ran out of my current Spanish vocabulary.

The bell to begin rang, and we women each chose a table with a number and two chairs: one for us, one for the potential matches. I took lucky number seven. Across the way, life was beautiful for the petite woman, who was already talking to a man who'd sat down. But at my table, life could have used some improving. My second chair was still empty.

The bell rang again, and then a man who appeared to be at least ten years out of the thirty-to-forty range sat down with a big smile. "*Hola*," he said. Seven minutes with man number one seemed like an eternity, especially when he switched from Spanish to English after I said I was American.

"I visit New York, yes," he said. "I help you with Spanish, you help me with English." He smiled just as the bell rang to change. I heard that line or a variation of it repeated ten times as many men wanted to help me with Spanish in exchange for help with English.

Out of the thirteen men, just two did not speak English or ask me to help them with English. I wasn't sure why those other eleven men thought a language exchange would be a romantic thing to propose. These unsolicited offers, with their unspoken ulterior motives, made me feel like I'd already been taken advantage of. More accurately, it could also be said that I couldn't see myself speaking the language of love with any of the men, either. And, since none of them were properly trained language teachers, I didn't want to imagine what they thought constituted a language exchange. If I needed help, I would ask for it.

When I returned to my apartment, I emailed the organizer my matches: the two men who did not speak English. On Sunday, the organizer wrote me back to see whether I wanted to change my mind. I replied no and ended up with one match, who sent me a LinkedIn request to connect which I marked as spam.

Chapter 10
Jardin de los Sueños

It had been a week and a half since Cristian left my apartment abruptly to go to the dinner party. If he'd been in the office last week or this week, he hadn't come over to say hello or ask whether we all wanted to go out to lunch. I rationalized this as that he knew I had so much work to do and really didn't want to bother me, since I was the only one to keep track of blog posts, keywords, contacting websites, and writing press releases.

In reality, all my projects were delayed since the release of the new version of the app was also behind schedule. Cristian and Alex didn't seem to mind and would always say it would be ready tomorrow, but it never was. And our online reviews made it clear to the world that the ParaLlevar app didn't work properly and would in fact uninstall itself.

This was something I hadn't even thought of before taking this job, and it was definitely not what I had imagined the job was going to be like. On one hand, I did what was asked of me and avoided questions like "when is the app going to work?" or "when is ParaLlevar going to make money?". Being a good team player meant I had to suck it up and if everyone worked hard enough, we'd all be successful if ParaLlevar was going to be the next big startup in a few years.

On the other, it was very frustrating to know that my marketing activities were promoting something that may not have a future. Everything was so uncertain. And it was a bit humiliating to think my MBA was being spent on getting people to install an app that didn't even do what it was supposed to.

"Hi, Sierra. You know we have been dedicated to working on the release of the new app, and I know we were supposed to meet today. Do you want to meet after work for happy hour with me and Fernando to celebrate? I can answer your questions then for the press release. We are going to push it live tomorrow or maybe next week. Hahaha. We still don't know exactly," Alex said.

"That's great news! Sure, let me know when you guys are going to go to happy hour. Is Cristian going to go?" I replied.

"Oh, probably not. He's been out this week because his wife's grandmother died. I think he'll be back next week. See you later."

And, with that, I turned to look at Jardin de los Sueños. I had now been in Madrid for almost a month. The first week was defined by getting acclimated; the second week, working; the third week, getting paid and having a lip-contact session with Cristian; and the fourth week, finding out he was married. I'd never seen him wear a ring. I wondered whether he was also hiding children. And I wondered the real reason why he kept the separate apartment.

Part of my hopes had now instantly disappeared almost like being totally erased from a chalkboard. I decided to take a break and go down to finally see what Jardin de los Sueños was all about. That store was representative of my hopes and expectations for being here. I wanted to live out my own garden of dreams by having Cristian as my boyfriend.

I kept looking at the pink window while crossing the street. To my surprise, it was like a Victoria's Secret, not a store for girls at all. I guess Jardin de los Sueños had some sexual connotation to it, although I wasn't sure whether I would ever be the type of woman to buy seductive lingerie for myself or have any man buy it for me at the rate my romantic life was going.

Inside, everything was pink from the carpet to the checkout area to the hangers, too. I looked at a few price tags. This place was expensive, charging 100 euros for bras and fifty euros for matching panties. I knew I should be using my money to pay off my loans for the next thirty years, not splurging on stuff no one was going to see. But, I figured, this was my break time, and I should make the most of it.

When I walked by the sale rack, I spotted a pajama set for only ten euros. The red shirt had a big gold heart on it, and the matching pants had smaller hearts. Probably they were left over from Valentine's Day. I would be the type of woman that buys Valentine's Day gifts for herself, albeit a little late. The pajamas looked like they would fit, and it was nice to be distracted materially for a moment with this super bargain.

After I paid for the pajamas, the cashier put them in a pink branded bag. I walked back into the office building, and the concierge gave me a rather strange smile. *Maybe now he will ask me to do a language exchange, too*, I thought sarcastically, as I raised my eyebrows the bitch way to say *no chance in hell*. I folded the bag and put it discreetly under my arm in the elevator. When I got to my desk, I put my new pajamas in my laptop bag and then tried to get back to work but kept on getting distracted by looking at the Jardin de los Sueños website and then searching for events happening tonight—mainly to meet men.

My mind raced back to the receipt that Cristian had taken out of the kitchen drawer. It was from Jardin de los Sueños for 250 euros. I now put two and two together, or in this case one and one together. He must have bought some lingerie there for his lover, who also stayed at the apartment from time to time. This was why the bed so was big in that apartment that was for "guests." And all this while his wife was with her sick grandmother. Now, with the news of her passing, I wondered what Cristian's next move would be.

"Ready, Sierra? Let's go celebrate with beer!" exclaimed Alex.

Chapter 11
Single Man's Projections

It was Alex, Fernando, and myself who were going to go grab a beer at a bar on the same block as the office. They were speaking in Spanish, which was too fast for my comprehension since I was still not registered for a Spanish class. I didn't have much interaction with Fernando on a daily basis, but I did know that he spoke at least some English. I hoped they would include me in the conversation once we got to the bar.

We entered and sat down at a table near the corner. It was an average bar that could have been anywhere in the world: loud, dirty, and crowded. They had TVs that were showing a soccer match, too. Alex ordered beer for us all without even asking whether I wanted a beer.

"You know, Sierra, we like you a lot better than Melinda. She would have never come out with us for a beer," said Fernando.

"Oh, really? I heard Melinda was an intern. Where did she go after she left ParaLlevar?" I asked, trying to be discreet.

"We don't know. I think she went back to America after she had a fight with Cristian. She came for three months just like you and stayed at the apartment," Fernando continued. The beers arrived along with a small bowl of peanuts.

"Well, startups aren't for everyone," Alex said,

quickly changing the topic, and took a giant gulp of his beer. He continued, "Sierra, I started working on some things for the press release for you to include like some new updates we made to the apps. Probably it will be live, at least in Google Play next week," he said as he took out a folded paper from his pocket.

Fernando took the paper, and then they both started speaking in Spanish again. I sat there drinking a beer, which made me want to vomit. I didn't like the taste of beer at all. I only pretended to like it because this was a work thing. Remembering that beer had some health benefits, I imagined it was a berry banana smoothie while the two discussed some tech-related things for what seemed like fifteen or twenty minutes. I was watching the TV closest to us to see some super hot guys playing soccer. I wondered whether any soccer players actually came to this bar.

Abruptly, Fernando got up, handed the paper back to Alex and said, "OK, see you guys. I have to go now to meet my girlfriend for dinner. Bye."

"Bye."

Alex turned back to me and gave me the paper. "Sierra, let me know if you have any questions. I can read your press release before you send it out to make sure you understood what we are doing," he said and waved over the server again to order another beer for himself. I declined beer number two. I still had more than three-quarters of my beer left.

"Thanks, Alex. I'll look at this tomorrow. Congrats on getting it all done. I did have a question about my job. I have two months left to stay in Madrid as a tourist. Do you know what will happen after that? I mean, with my job at ParaLlevar?"

"I don't know about that. Cristian has been trying to hire Americans because he says he likes their work ethic, but I also think he just likes American girls, too. In my opinion, I think you American girls are all the same," Alex said as he took a sip of beer number two.

"Oh, really?" I said, trying to flirt with a smile at the corner of my mouth. I now took a couple of sips of my beer to mirror Alex. If he cut his long hair, he would be much more attractive in a manly way, and maybe he just needed a nice girlfriend to help him with things like this. My desperation was surfacing more and more with the beer that now was almost gone in an attempt at both flirting and fitting in.

Alex was a good-looking, smart guy whom I wouldn't mind dating. And, since married Cristian was dealing with family issues, I thought I would again try to get my meat where I got my bread. I knew that it was pathetic and I was doing exactly what one is not supposed to do. But I felt like I had more freedom now that I was in Madrid, where I didn't understand social norms, and so I figured I might as well do what I wanted instead of trying to guess what I should be doing.

"You all have some things in common. You come here to Madrid and think it's different for you."

"What do you mean?" Now this was not flirting but general investigation. Not only had I not registered for a Spanish class, but I also still didn't understand much about Spanish culture, especially relationships between men and women, romantic and otherwise.

"Pretty girls have the most problems," he continued cryptically.

"OK, what do these girls have in common?"

"You live like the show *Sex and the City*. That was the problem with Melinda. She came here and didn't work much, just spent all her time with Cristian. She stayed at the apartment you are staying at and went shopping all the time."

"I don't know what you are talking about. I never watched that show."

"I thought everyone watched that show. Well, you spend money on clothes from famous brands and want someone rich and then richer to get the richest man you can just to have a poor man on the side to please you. You know, the woman *always* chooses. But she did not choose Cristian. That's why she got fired."

I exploded at his revelation. "Alex, I'm not sure what I am choosing here besides to have a conversation with a man that is projecting an American show's values on a confused woman in her twenties that has had one serious relationship with a man I was in love with and that was not because of his bank account. And, by the way, I'm not sure if this is in any American show you watch, but I have to keep on working to pay off my student loans until I'm probably fifty. Do you know how much debt I'm in from school and my credit cards?" My debt problem had reared its ugly, angry head, which was taboo and tacky at the same time. Coupled with my romantic yearnings and culture shock, this was a toxic cocktail for everyone.

But instead of trying to defuse the situation, Alex asked, "And your parents don't care that you are here in Spain having fun instead of working in America?"

"I'm not sure what you expected, but no, I'm not having fun now and haven't since I got here. I don't understand the Spanish language well, and I obviously don't understand Spanish culture. Or why romantic language exchanges are so popular. Furthermore, I have a job here, and my parents have nothing to do with my decision. I think it's best if we call it a night and say goodbye now. I'll see you Monday in the office." And with that, I stood up and left the bar.

Chapter 12
Expats

Still reeling from the blowup over beers, I now knew firsthand what culture shock really meant. It was more than a disorientation and frustration in an unfamiliar environment, as I had read on expat websites. It was the personal realization that there was a big difference in social norms, work behaviors, and relationships with my colleagues that would come up in unexpected ways. Struggling on a deeper level with how to handle the differences was painful. The stressful environment of the startup and being on a small team seemed to magnify imperfections and morph my culture shock into a split personality.

And now I knew what at least one of my colleagues thought of me: an American woman in Madrid out to get a rich man and live like the show *Sex and the City*. I thought only serial brunch-eating women of a certain demographic watched that show, but now, fifteen years after its heyday, Spanish men—or at least one—were fans, too.

Focusing on my financial goals and leaving my culture-shocked persona out of the workplace was the best thing I could do. By now, February was almost over. I had been working occasionally with Alex and Fernando only; Cristian was hardly in the office and would show up from time to time just for team meetings. Almost two months of not having to pay rent also allowed me to make more loan payments and put some money into my savings account, just in case this job ended in one month. There had been no evaluation or meeting about extending my three-month trial period.

One night, walking home from work, I saw a few people huddled around a large trash can on the curb. They were speaking in English, and my mood lifted. Maybe they needed some help; I definitely needed some conversation with native English speakers.

"Hey, guys. What's going on?" I asked.

"What does it look like?" blurted out a nondescript, brown-haired guy with a slight East Coast accent I couldn't place. "If you want anything, you better hurry up."

"What is this?" I said, looking into the trash can.

"It's from that organic store over there. This stuff never sells because it's too expensive, and then they throw it out on certain days. It's good. Don't worry; you won't get sick if you eat it right away. At least we haven't gotten sick from it, and we've been doing this for a while."

I was now shopping in the dumpster with the three other Americans. Maybe I could be friends with these expats. They seemed to know how to save money, and getting food out of a grocery store's trash seemed like only one step down from day-old food.

More people were now showing up, and I was jostled out of my spot while deciding whether I wanted the tofu dogs or the veggie burgers. Stepping back I held both packages and then wondered whether I would get sick. It was in the dirty trash can, after all, and the veggie burger box was slightly open. I wondered why the store just didn't donate this stuff or, if it was really an organic store, why they didn't compost some of it.

I put the two boxes back in the pile, and they were quickly snatched up. I saw a magazine off to the side and took that to read later.

"Come back next week. Same time, same place," said the East Coast guy. It seemed like he wanted to be friends.

"Maybe. Hey, why do you do this?"

"Why not? Everyone's gotta hustle. You probably have loans to pay off, too," he said and then went back to fishing out more bent boxes.

Maybe these people were the same people that my friend Jennifer had told me about before I left San Francisco. These people left the U.S. because they had too many student loans and never paid them off. Escaping to other countries and leaving their debt behind was what they did.

This could be my new life, if I wanted it. But that, to me, was the absolute worst-case scenario for not being able to afford anything let alone food. I was stunned when I thought about it: I'd experienced how it would feel to have no choice besides dumpster diving if I wanted to eat like a normal person. Having friends who ate garbage was not appealing to me, nor was shopping in a dumpster.

Chapter 13
How to Join a Cult

There was a yoga center advertised in the eco-friendly magazine I picked up from the dumpster. The ad showed a very nice, long white building surrounded by trees. *Now that would be a great weekend escape to get out of the city and be in nature for a weekend*, I thought. And this could be my reward for starting that online Spanish course last week. I decided to just do it and sent an email making a reservation for the coming weekend and locking in the eighty-five-euro special.

The email confirmation had all the details about the train and the bus I was advised to take from Madrid. It wasn't that far outside the city limits, just a little complicated to get to. I left that Friday after work with my backpack and took the train and the bus according to the email's instructions. A woman about my mom's age named Luz picked me up in a Jeep from the bus stop. She was very friendly and apologized for not knowing any English.

As we drove into the night, Luz spoke about the retreat center in Spanish loudly and slowly. One moment we were on a road, and the next moment I felt the car turn onto a surface that resembled the moon. It was very rocky with some craters that we had to slow down to navigate. All the while, Luz kept on talking as if everything were normal. I understood some words and was able to have a basic conversation about my life and job, but I wasn't sure how to ask why we were not on a road anymore.

We finally got to the yoga center, and even though it was dark, it looked exactly the same as the picture in the ad. The air was unpolluted, and the clear night sky hosted the stars, showing off their brilliance. After Luz parked, she went up to the door and opened it slowly and I followed.

The evening meditation was already in progress as we quietly entered. Everyone was wearing white and faced an altar with a cross. It reminded me of the chapel at my Catholic grade school. I took a seat and realized I was wearing all black. I sat there with my eyes open staring at the altar. I began to repeat a truth-seeking mantra: "What am I doing here?" The leader of the group, who was seated in the front, used a Tibetan singing bowl to bring the attention back to himself. My eyes were still glued to the altar.

The leader began talking about something spiritual. I was not engaging in the discussion and thought I would plead, "*no entiendo*," if someone uttered my name. But my resistance to group partic-ipation slowly eroded as I heard a word repeated several times: *obesidad*.

Being the representative of the most obese nation, it was my responsibility to clear the air before anything was said that was incorrect. I summa-rized in Spanglish for the group that people overeat primarily because they are lacking in self-love.

Since the American society is focused so much on material possessions, the heart and emotions are not fully expressed, which lead to disease. People don't care about themselves; they care about their things like electronics, cars and houses. But the complicated part is that being depressed, lonely, and full of anxiety both cause and are caused by poor food choices. I ended my summary with the observation that it's a vicious cycle, and fat shaming perpetuates the problem.

After my declaration, the leader said that he watches people at the supermarket buy food. The discussion was now veering to a documentary like *Super Size Me*. And at first I thought he was joking when he said he wanted to educate people at the supermarket about what to eat, but I soon realized that he was not. All the talk about food was making my stomach gurgle louder, and finally the discussion ended with a group hug and the secret handshake of the yoga center, which involved holding up three fingers.

Chapter 14
Potential Husband

The preparation of dinner was underway, and I noticed there was an older gentleman in his 70s talking with a woman about my age. I thought it would be a good idea for me to interrupt and introduce myself to them, make small talk, and be a friendly American. But it then dawned on me from the way they said "we" that they were a married couple and lived at the yoga center. Dinner seemed to take ages, and I ran out of things to say while my brain processed the unconventional relationship.

I went into the kitchen to check on dinner's status with my head whirling, stomach gurgling, and heart pounding. The group consisted of older men with younger women, special handshakes, and secret codes. Luz was the only older woman out of the group of twelve. I did a bizarre, clumsy U-turn out of the kitchen and went to the bathroom.

Something is not right here, I told myself and hoped there wasn't a camera in the stall. *But you are stuck here with no cell reception until Sunday.* My palms were now on the back of the stall door, and my head was hanging in between my arms. Goosebumps elevated my arm hair without me even noticing. The floor of the bathroom looked to be from the 1950s, and I wondered whether this place had been a prison before because it sure seemed to have been built for that.

Someone entered the bathroom and took the stall next to mine. It could have been the leader, for all I knew. I wiped my face off with the bottom of my T-shirt and opened the stall door. I washed my hands and exited as if everything was normal.

Taking a seat at the dinner table, now featuring some unidentifiable mush, I looked at another young woman with an older man at the table. There was another older man with a bald head who declared himself single and unemployed after he introduced himself. Was he going to be my husband for the weekend or for life if I didn't make it out of here on Sunday?

I moved seats to protect myself from any suitors or otherwise creepy people. I sat at the very end of the table with an empty chair on either side. I knew I was acting strange, but I could blame it on cultural differences.

After the discussion about obesity, I was hungry. I was very hungry. I helped myself to the mushy dish that they had prepared and, to my surprise, enjoyed it. However, I was not ready for another discussion they must have prepared along with dinner. The side of discussion started about God and creation and then went to the granular level of how being single destroys humanity and finished with putting me—at the head of the table, with two empty chairs on either side—on the spot by asking me, "*¿Por qué no estás casada?*" There was too much to try to explain, and culturally I wasn't sure these people would understand. I simplified my answer to "*No entiendo.*"

After the dishes were washed, I went straight to my room and was thankful there was a hot shower that night. The next day was more of the same with the fifty questions about spirituality after meals, but the hot water had "run out." And it was somehow always my turn in the newcomer spotlight to explain my thoughts and beliefs. By this point, I was over it. An older member took off his shirt and threw it at me during yoga as some type of territory-marking ritual. When the yoga class was over, I grabbed the smelly shirt with my pinky, then threw it away and went outside. I heard some gunshots and thought either this was hunting season or someone had just tried to escape this center. I couldn't be sure.

It was finally time to go. I was packed and asked for a ride to the bus stop at 9:00 AM. However, I was told I had to wait until after the vegetarian paella lunch was finished. Then, the leader said, I needed to pay. Despite being agitated and anxious to leave, I smiled and asked how much the total was, and to my surprise, there had been a price surge while I was at the yoga center. It was not the eighty-five euros listed on the website; now it was 150 euros. This was a case of spiritual extortion. I smiled again and thought, *I could get mad, but in reality, I am paying for my freedom.* I sat down to eat my last meal of vegetarian paella, which was really yellow rice with peas and a cut-up tomato.

The vegetarian paella was in my stomach, my money was in the organizers' hands, and two men were in the car waiting for me. I thought nothing of it and only was visualizing getting on the bus. With the faked pleasantries of small talk all the way to the bus stop making me a bit nervous, reality was slowly sinking in with every word they were saying. This was now an attempt at trust building or, worse, coercion. The men didn't leave me alone at the bus stop, but rather proceeded to get out of the car and stand on either side of me. I grabbed my suitcase from the one man, and all three of us walked to the bus door. I tried my best to say goodbye, but before I knew it, I was not alone as I turned to go up the bus stairs.

My heart almost exploded as the leader came closer from behind and touched my shoulder as I was trying to find a seat. I turned around and he gave me an unreciprocated, unusually long hug and said he hoped to see me again. My intuition wasn't wrong. They were trying to get me to go back with them to the yoga center.

I said thank you and sat down next to a young woman after he put my suitcase in the rack above. He said another goodbye and stayed on the bus. Finally, he left the bus after the driver said something to him. I stood up to see them both standing off to the side watching as the bus pulled away.

Chapter 15
El Tercer Mes

It was a relief that on Monday, no one showed up to the office. For the better part of the morning, I sat at my desk looking out the window at the people below and surfing the Internet to see whether there was anything about that cult that was public either in English or Spanish, until Alex came to my desk. He told me about a big meeting we were going to have next week, which would include everyone on the team, except me, and some potential investors.

It no longer seemed like Cristian was in charge of the startup. Alex was the one running the show and giving me new tasks all the time. Now, I had to write some presentation to detail all the marketing activities I had been doing so Alex could present it to the investors. Since this meeting was supposed to have happened in January and since the new version of the app was behind schedule, everyone had to make their best effort, especially since the office was going to be closed for Easter in a few weeks.

That reminded me: I had to figure out what Lexie was planning on doing. After a weekend where I could have ended up in a cult and married to some old man for the rest of my life, everything seemed so mundane. *Yes, of course, you and Mario can stay with me*, my email to Lexie said. *I'd be thrilled to finally meet him after hearing so much about him.*

Throughout the week, the weather actually got a bit colder, instead of getting warmer for spring. On Thursday, when I got home from work, I flipped the light switch to find out that there was no power in my apartment. I checked the other light switches and the fridge, and everything was out. I found the box of switches but didn't know where to begin. I decided to call Cristian. As much as I didn't want him to come over, he had to fix this. I left a message for him, then I started to make a salad.

Just five minutes into dinner preparation, I heard forceful knocking and then, "Hi, Sierra. It's me, Cristian. I can help turn the lights on," came through the door.

I got up to open the door and saw him for the first time in two weeks. It was also the first time I had seen him not dressed up but instead in jeans and what looked like a ski jacket. He had dark circles under his eyes, and his hair needed a good wash.

"Hi, Cristian. That was fast. Thank you," I said nonchalantly.

"Well, I fix things in this old building, too. Since it's my father's building, I know a lot about it, and I like to help out when I can," he said, not looking at me but going straight to the fuse box. He flipped a few switches back and forth, and then the lights went on and the fridge started humming.

"Are you hungry, Sierra? Let's go to dinner

because we haven't talked much these last few weeks, and I'm sorry about this power outage."

"OK, that's nice. Maybe you can tell me about the meeting next week, too," I replied as I got my jacket. It was a relief that he was not dressed up because now I didn't feel fashionably inferior. As our first official outing together in Madrid, he was taking me out to dinner, and we'd be seen together in a public place. This was huge and maybe a second chance that now he was going to take a romantic relationship more seriously with me.

To avoid the forced intimacy of the tiny elevator, we took the stairs. Then we walked into a restaurant that was just a few storefronts down from the building. It looked very traditional, and Cristian greeted everyone in the restaurant with two kisses, smiles, and a few laughs. He led the way to the back table and asked me what I wanted. I told him I really wanted to try authentic, non-vegetarian paella; Cristian said that was a good choice and then ordered it for us.

Cristian told me more about the meeting in a few weeks and said that I needed to think about going back in April and getting a work visa, if I wanted to keep my job with ParaLlevar. Even if the investors didn't want to invest, he would continue to fund it himself as he was sure that it would take off. He even said that the restaurant we were in was excited to begin delivering with ParaLlevar and the owner had started to take English lessons to prepare for the orders from expats. That was not in line with my initial fantasy of climbing the social ladder. Maybe he didn't have as much money or class as I had thought. He certainly didn't have as much romantic *savoir faire* as I would have hoped.

There were no signs that Cristian was going to hit on me again or talk about his wife. He did order wine with the paella, and I didn't think anything of it. The wine came and then the paella, which was so much better than the vegetarian version I had when I was at the cult headquarters. Every bite was full of surprises: chicken, mussels, calamari rings, and shrimp.

I was very much focused on eating when Cristian started, "You know, Sierra, I've been wanting to tell you more about Melinda. She was the one who got this job started for you. She was very intelligent and made a lot of good things happen for us before you got here. I admire how brave you Americans are and also how you approach work."

"Thanks for the compliment. Yes, her work has helped me a great deal. What is she doing now, and why didn't she want to continue working?"

"Melinda and I had a difference of opinion."

"Oh, OK," I said, thinking that was a bizarre way to end that part of the conversation. The dinner concluded with a coffee, and then Cristian walked me back to the building. He stopped at the door and looked at me.

"Sierra, we are very happy you are here. I also wanted to tell you that…"

"Cristian, ¡*tanto tiempo*!" exclaimed an elderly man who was approaching the door. A short conversation in Spanish took place between the two of them while I stood smiling a polite smile.

After a few minutes, the old man left, and Cristian turned to me and said, "He's a good man. What was I saying before we met him?"

"I think it's time for me to go up to the apartment. Thanks for dinner and everything," I said awkwardly.

"Oh, yes, I wanted to tell you that after that meeting with the investors, we'll talk about the next steps for your job. I wish you a good night, Sierra," he said and then gave me two kisses. I went up to the apartment feeling glad but a little sad that there wasn't a second attempt at a romantic overture.

Chapter 16
An English Vacation

Easter was coming up, and I took some extra time off to make it two weeks of freedom from the office. The downside was that I was working as a freelancer so I would not get paid for those two weeks. Madrid and the cult headquarters were the only places I had visited, and I wanted to see more of Spain. I also wanted to get away from the startup and take a break.

Financially, I could afford not to work for a couple weeks because I was caught up on all my loan and credit card payments. My debt was nowhere near being paid off but taking two weeks off wasn't going to impact my bank account that much.

Still, just like the cheap millionaires who used coupons that I'd heard about, I knew I had to save the money I did have. When I was conducting the new business development research on expat sites, I discovered an article about volunteering on your next vacation. One online ad described an opportunity that was exclusively free for English speakers—all expenses were included except transportation to a small town in the south of Spain, near Alicante. I had visions of the beach and palm trees dancing in my head, so I decided to apply.

Even though this trip was free for English speakers, there were still some responsibilities tied to the vacation. The tradeoff was that I would have to speak with native Spanish speakers who were learning English from 9:00 AM to 9:00 PM every day.

After a fifteen-minute interview, the one-week-long, free working vacation was all mine. The program accepted me, and I made the appropriate arrangements to arrive the day it started. But I didn't look at a map until I was ready to get on the bus to leave for the hotel. It turned out that the hotel was two hours away from everything: beaches, human contact, and shopping. I would be secluded in this hotel for the next week with a bunch of people I had never met before.

When I finally arrived at the hotel, the lobby's white marble floors and turquoise sofas with yellow pillows greeted me with a friendly, four-star vibe. My room had a huge king-size bed, and I even had a bathtub with jets. Everything was nicer than Cristian's studio apartment.

After putting my suitcase on the foldable luggage rack and reapplying my lip gloss, I went downstairs for the opening session. The seat where my nametag was placed was next to a few other people. As I sat down, I began to look around to examine who I would spend the week with. This could have been some type of reality show setup with a wide variety of ages and backgrounds. There were three out of fifty people who looked to be around my age.

A very tan, leathery-skinned blonde woman was sitting next to me. Her name was Kat, and she had a strong English accent. She was with her husband, Sean, who had thinning gray hair and also was leatherlike in appearance. They explained to me that they were here to do the same job I was going to do and that they were retired school-teachers who now lived in Spain and taught English when they could. "We're English pensioners living in Benidorm now and have all the time in the world but just not all the money." She began laughing. I was shocked to know that my money issues could linger into retirement and that I could end up doing free vacations into my sixties.

"This is our seventh time doing this, so if you have any questions, ask us," Kat whispered in my ear and then gave me a wink. I was unable to introduce myself as they smiled and then turned to look at the director who had already started speaking.

The director was cheerfully explaining the roles of all the native English speakers. We each had a Spanish buddy to help with English and ensure that they were practicing the language over the week. My buddy was María José, an adver-tising executive from outside Madrid who was not wearing a wedding band. I had seen her type before in Madrid: early 50s, dark brown hair with blonde highlights, an affinity for perfume, lots of makeup, and a love of cigarettes. She was impeccably dressed with a fitted coral dress and matching coral shoes. When she introduced herself to me, I could tell she was trying her best to use the English that she could remember, but what came out was, "Hi. I María José. This is very funny. I going to speak English with you, OK?"

Since she was my buddy, I had to make sure she was speaking English at all times. *This may be painful*, I thought after listening to her introduction. Furthermore, María José had to prepare a ten-minute presentation with my help on any topic she chose. She was very nice and polite, which made up for my lack of patience and initiative in correcting her as the week went on.

Dinner time was something to look forward to, I soon learned. Every night we had different assigned seats, and almost every night someone asked something inappropriate and impolite. I had to smile every time someone asked me how old I was or whether I had a boyfriend. The first day, I made up some garbage about the right one not finding me. On day two, I was self-conscious about being asked this and decided to respond that I had been recently released from jail and didn't have much of a social life. The English speakers laughed; the Spanish speakers got quiet. Good old María José was the only Spanish speaker to know I was kidding and said, "*Guapa*, you are crazy like me. That is why you are single."

The last day arrived, and as she prepared her presentation about "gin and tonics," I couldn't help but stare at her trying to type with her long finger-nails. She put some sexist pictures of women in low-cut dresses and men in suits drinking at a bar as the first slide in her PowerPoint. "Gin and tonic help you relax and make you feel sexy," she said. I helped her with the intro and was happy that she got it almost right. She did a good job and really put a lot of effort into having fun with English.

At the end of the program, at graduation, María José gave me a card. She asked me whether I wanted to come to teach English at her company for a few hours a day. It would be until June, and then they stopped the lessons for July and August. María José said I would get paid in cash and I didn't need a work visa. I said I would think about it. I honestly never thought I would be qualified to teach English. And why would I waste my MBA on teaching English anyway? I was already wasting it at ParaLlevar.

Chapter 17
Third Wheel

When I got home from Alicante, I had to prepare the apartment for Lexie and Mario's arrival the next day. Going against my previous reservations, I agreed to let them stay with me for the three nights they would be in Madrid. I knew they didn't have much money, and it wasn't even my apartment, so everyone should share in my good luck before it was over in two weeks when my tourist visa expired.

Since I was still single, I also mentally prepared myself for being the third wheel. There was no need for me to feel embarrassed about being single or inferior because of my debt, I reasoned with myself. I didn't want to be single, just like I didn't want to be in debt. I had been saving as much money as I could while working the past three months and knew I was making an effort to learn Spanish, meet new people, and have experiences I couldn't have in the U.S. I reassured myself that it would be great to see Lexie and meet Mario; after all, if everyone liked him, I probably would like him, too.

As a good big sister, I went to the airport to meet them. I had been running late and just threw on my black spandex workout pants and an oversized sweatshirt. I wasn't too concerned with what I looked like; I just wanted to see my sister.

When I saw Lexie, I immediately knew she was in love. She looked amazing, with her long, straight hair hanging now past her shoulders and her trendy, extra-large cardigan and black calf boots. Mario was pushing two suitcases with a smile on his face. He had a round baby face, dimples I could see from here, and a chubby body with short dark wavy hair. Although he was a little on the small side, he was a lot cuter than any other guy she'd ever dated. I waved at them, and Lexie started running.

"SIERRAAAA!" she yelled as she gave me a bear hug.

"I'm so happy you are here! You look gorgeous! How are you doing? How was the flight?" I said, a bit nervous, but also elated to have reconnected with her. She seemed to be excelling at life and looking great, and I didn't know how to tell her about my unstable job and Cristian.

"Sierra, this is Mario. Mario, this is my sister you finally get to meet!" Lexie said.

"Hi, Sierra. Very nice to finally meet you. We are happy to be here and thanks for letting us stay at your place and of course, meeting us here, too!" said Mario as he held out his hand for a handshake. He was like a little angel with his dimples and sincerity.

"My pleasure! I'm happy to have you both here and show you around. Let's go back to my apartment and put your stuff there and then we can go eat something."

"Sierra, I want to take you to my friend's bar. He's expecting us today. It's nice. They have a real

Italian *aperitivo* you can try. I'm sure you will like it."

And with that, we got on the metro, went back to my apartment, and then raced off to the Italian bar Mario's friend owned. I was happy he had a plan, and he also seemed to know Madrid fairly well. I wondered how he knew so many Italians and his way around Madrid, so I asked him once we were inside the bar and after Mario ordered us all a drink called spritz.

"Mario, how do you know so many people in Madrid? And how do you know your way around the city so well?"

"My cousin used to live here, and I visited him before I came to Michigan."

"Oh, nice. Thanks for suggesting this place. I have never been here before. So how much longer do you have in school?" I had no idea how long he had been dating Lexie or what he was even studying. I knew Lexie was trying to graduate this summer but also had to ask whether that was still happening, too.

"I'm finishing up my master's in biology, and I hope to graduate in December. Look, we can go to the buffet over there. It's free, you know," he said with a smile.

"And I will graduate in August, and Mom and Dad are throwing a big party for me. You have to come, Sierra. I'm so excited to finish school," Lexie said as she did a little dance and pounded on my shoulder. We all went up to the buffet that had pasta, salad, and some fried balls.

"That's great, Lexie! Of course I'll try to make it back home in August. Have you started looking for a job yet? You know, paying off your loans is really hard. We should talk about what you'll do after you graduate," I said casually, then, turning to Mario, I said, "Mario, what are these fried balls?"

"Oh, those are *arancini*, and Mario makes the best recipe. Yeah, I know about the job thing. But I don't have as many loans as you do, so I don't have to worry as much," Lexie said as she rubbed Mario's back with her left hand while her right hand held a plate piled high with pasta.

We walked back to sit down and eat. I wanted Lexie to know that she did have to worry and that her degree in international relations wasn't a sure-fire degree for any job. I knew she didn't have as many loans as me, but I also wondered whether she viewed Mario as her long-term meal ticket. Sure, he knew where to get free food in Madrid, but was that enough? So just like the woman on the plane, I was about to offer some unsolicited advice.

"Yeah, Lexie, I know you're not in the same position as me. But it took me more than a year to get a job after I got my MBA, and it's not easy to sort out how you are going to eat and pay your bills when you have no job or have to take a minimum-wage job. It's one of the reasons why I'm in Madrid because I got the job here to help me pay off my loans," I said, taking the first sip of my spritz, which was fizzy, bitter, and a weirdly bright orange.

"I get it. I'll look for a job after we get back from Italy! I have to go to the bathroom now." In typical Wellington fashion, she abruptly cut the conversation short, ignored my big-sister-soapbox speech, stood up, kissed Mario on the top of his head, and pranced off to the bathroom as if nothing was ever going to stop her from going to the bathroom or wherever she wanted to go.

"Sierra, look, no one on the outside cares about your loans, except maybe your bank. We know you are smart, with your MBA, so you should be able to find a way to pay off your loans and get on with your life," Mario said in a more direct way than I had anticipated. His spritz was almost gone. He continued, "I think you are different than most Americans for taking a big risk and coming to Europe to work. But you seem so focused on your finances. Do you ever want to settle down and have a boyfriend?"

"You know, I'm not sure. I'm confused about relationships and my finances. While all these people in Madrid have more strollers than I've ever seen in my life, I have two suitcases on wheels and a lot of debt. Would my future husband pay off my debt? I have no idea. But what I'm really trying to say is that I can't get a date who's not married." I stopped my confession and avoided Mario's eye contact.

"There is this saying I like: Love is like a shadow. Love could find you when you are not looking. That is what happened when I met Lexie. But don't you think you are obsessed with these loans? It sounds like they are taking over your life," he said.

Lexie now came back from the bathroom and gave Mario a kiss on the cheek. "What are you guys talking about?"

"Finances," I replied as I took another bite of the wonderful pasta and gave a fake smile with my mouth full at Lexie and Mario.

Chapter 18
Sister to Sister

The seriousness of Mario gave way to a more playful side as we started telling funny stories and talked about his first impressions of Detroit. After two more rounds of spritz and many more trips to the buffet, we left the restaurant barely able to walk. The jet lag was setting in for Mario and Lexie, and I was just exhausted from the working vacation. We ended up taking a cab back to my apartment, which Mario paid for, and then all three of us collapsed on the double bed for a good hour before Mario started to snore. At that point, I got the sofa bed ready, and they went to their corner of the apartment, and I reclaimed my bed all to myself.

I woke up hearing the shower running. Then I turned over to see Lexie standing over me and then shaking the bed saying "earthquake" like we used to do when we were kids. Now we were both laughing hysterically, and she collapsed next to me, still laughing.

"*Buenosssssss díassss, señorita,*" I said in an exaggerated way.

"*Buongiorno, signorina,*" she replied back.

"What do you want to do today?" I asked her.

"Hang out with you. Mario is going to meet some more friends and I think his cousin for lunch, and then we can meet up with him later in the day.

What do you think about shopping or going to a museum?"

My sister had definitely changed. She started out just five minutes ago as the hyper, attention-seeking little sister and then shifted into a mature, schedule-making adult who surprisingly wanted to make time for me and not spend all her time attached to her boyfriend.

Mario came out of the bathroom, clean, dressed, and smelling good. "Hi, Wellington sisters!" he said with a smile that lit up the room. He was not human. Saying cute things, looking good, getting us free food—it wasn't normal for any guy around our age to have so many amazing things to offer.

Lexie sat up, and I followed suit. "Hey Mario, we're going to hang out today while you catch up with your friends. Then we'll meet you back here later on in the day, say, 5:00, OK?"

"OK, that sounds good."

"Sierra, I almost forgot. Mom gave me a package for you," Lexie said while walking back to her suitcase. She took out a large padded envelope, and I wondered what was in it.

I opened the package to see a few pieces of mail. There was an envelope with Bev's name and an address in Brooklyn. Even before I read her card, I had a feeling I knew what happened: that she'd had to move back to Brooklyn because she couldn't find a place. I opened her letter first to learn that she moved at the end of January to Brooklyn. But she wasn't living with her son. He'd found a studio for her near his brownstone, so she was able to keep living on her own, which she was thrilled about. I was happy for her.

Lexie and I left the apartment and walked down Calle Ibiza to enter Retiro Park. We were immediately approached by an African man asking us in English whether we needed anything. It was one of those trigger questions that ended up activating a part of my brain that was in need and in want of many things. I veered my thoughts away from the lonely, isolated, desperated part of my brain to the present moment of his park business. Grabbing Lexie, who was smiling and starting to say, "No, thank...," I walked quickly past, stuffed the emotion back where it came from, and did not say anything.

"That's the first black man I've seen since I got here. Why did he ask if we needed anything?" she whispered as we were walking away.

"Most black people I see here in Madrid I think come from Africa somewhere. They always seem to be begging outside supermarkets or here in the park. I don't really know if he is selling drugs or something else," I explained.

Happy families and kids seemed to multiply. Lovers having intimate picnics on too-small blankets were everywhere, about to procreate publicly. A myriad of cyclists was competing for asphalt. It was a typical day at the park, and we were two American tourists soaking it all up.

After we exited the park, we continued on Calle de Alcalá, and Lexie exclaimed, "Wow, look at that huge angel! Madrid is so beautiful and magical!"

"Yeah, sometimes. I think Madrid is loud and obnoxious. Plus everyone is always in a group. But the worst is how many people get drunk and make out on the metro on Friday and Saturday nights. Come on, *hermana*, let's go to Puerta del Sol, but first I need to show you the ham museum," I said laughing.

Lexie was confused and shocked at the ham legs dangling from the ceiling. Her confusion soon disappeared after we had some wine and paper-thin slices of *jamón serrano*. She took pictures of the ham legs, us and the ham legs, and then a very handsome employee holding some ham.

On the way back to my apartment, I asked her, sister to sister, "Is it really serious between you two?"

"Oh, you know, I don't know. I'm just about having fun, but I do like him a lot, and everyone else tells me how lucky I am because he is so incredible."

"Why does it matter what everyone else thinks of the guy you are with? But really, how does Mario treat you? He is intelligent, good looking, and funny, but that's only what I see. My wish for you is that he or any man you are with is honest, respectful, and serious enough to be the man you deserve," I said, hoping that my support of her in a healthy relationship would be noted and appreciated. I also wanted to tell her about Cristian, but I was really embarrassed to say that I had a crush on and had lip contact with a married man, which was not a mistake I wanted my sister to ever make.

After much walking around and shopping, we headed back to the apartment ahead of our 5:00 deadline to meet Mario. Mario seemed too good to be true. He was funny and cool in addition to being very smart and caring, not only for my sister but also for me. I wasn't sure whether he was always like this or whether it was an act.

My Mom's words ran through my head: "Everyone loves Mario." He had to have some weakness that would make him unlikable, but I couldn't find it after hosting them. My sister looked very happy although a bit delusional, and that could have been love's effect on her. It was my responsibility to watch out for her, and part of me thought that she'd come to Madrid to get my approval. This relationship could be very long term for Lexie and our family, if it was as serious as I had a feeling it could be.

Chapter 19
Demoted

I thought Lexie was going to ask me how long I was going to stay in Madrid and what I was going to do next before she and Mario left to go to Italy, but she didn't. They left the next day and seemed super-happy and grateful to me for letting them stay.

A few hours after they left, I stood in front of the bathroom mirror. What the fuck was I doing feeling underemployed at some quasi-internship in Madrid with a rich man that I wanted something to happen with all the while staying in the mistress's apartment and attempting to function in a foreign language? I felt like my life wasn't real. Real people had real jobs, friends, and families. I had two suitcases and watched reality TV to understand what the majority of people were doing in life. And most people were probably living a happy life like my sister.

That evening, I got an email from Jennifer saying I had to make a decision about my six boxes that were at her place soon because she was going to be moving in with her boyfriend in May. I presumed this was the same guy she had started to date before I got to San Francisco, whom I never met. With everything that had been going on the past couple of months, I had almost forgotten about those boxes and what was in them. It was nice that she offered to pay for shipping to my parents' house in Detroit since she understood my situation. But the email was so dry and formal, like a legal brief, that I started thinking more about our friendship.

Our friendship had changed over the past months, and instead of it getting stronger when I moved to San Francisco where she had already been living for a few years, it had fallen apart. I wanted to break up with her. At the root of my decision was jealousy. I was envious of her family paying her loans and of her lawyer job in San Francisco. Now, she was moving on in life to live with a boyfriend. My jealous mind jumped ahead to the nice apartment they would get, probably in Pacific Heights, and I pictured the white fluffy rug, huge windows with a great view of the Golden Gate Bridge, and marble countertops. She had a real life, and I wasn't included.

I was fast becoming an underachieving friend with no good job, no fancy friends, and no place to call home, which contributed to my demotion in Jennifer's friend hierarchy. I knew her values well enough to make this assessment. Indeed, I never thought friends would dump other friends for being underachievers. I'd had to search online to learn about relationships post-college. From what I read, it seemed that both guys and girls would also dump each other when dating if they thought the other one was an underachiever.

I went back to the bathroom mirror to face myself for the second time in one day. I shifted my mindset from how you were ranked by GPA when you applied to college and business school, to how you were ranked as an adult—by job title, salary, neighborhood, romantic competency, and appearance.

My life had become a series of poor choices that left me out of the status quo. No one ever said "stay single and unemployed" instead, they always said shit like "working is not working if you do what you love" and "you'll find the right one someday." Yet here I was, having failed again at a job where they thought I was an intern and unsuccessfully tried to pursue romance with the boss. But, what really was bothering me was being single in Madrid where families and couples were everywhere. I felt like Quasimodo's identical twin but at least I had an MBA.

Easter was now over, and after celebrating the Resurrection, I got an epiphany: Perhaps my triumph would be posthumous. This was a bit too hard to handle, so I refocused on the miracle of the Resurrection. I'd always believed in miracles, so now, I focused on manifesting some miracle to make myself into a real adult. I did the mature thing and wrote Jennifer back a nice email thanking her for her generosity and accepting the offer to have her ship my boxes back to Detroit. I then sent an email to my parents saying six boxes were on their way.

Chapter 20
A Proposal

Walking to work the Tuesday after Easter break, I started to tear up because I was now more homesick and isolated than ever. I pulled myself together by the time I walked into an empty office, which seemed a bit unusual. I had to turn on all the lights. Then I took out my computer and checked my email. Cristian had sent me a meeting invite for 4:00 PM, which I accepted and then started to look at airfare back to Detroit in between writing blog posts for April. A harder-to-swallow reality was sinking in after the time off, and I didn't know what I was doing with my life here in Madrid or at this job.

But my responsibilities didn't stop and now that vacation was over, I was still responsible for the recurring tasks. Things were up in the air about whether I would be able to stay past the three-month mark. There had been no major announcements about the product or funding, and things kept on being the same as they were when I arrived in January.

When it was 4:00, I walked to Cristian's office to find him sitting at his desk, working diligently on his computer.

"Hi, Sierra. How are you? Please sit down and give me a minute."

I sat. It felt strange to be sitting in silence and looking down at my notebook.

"OK, Sierra. I hope you had a nice Easter break. Let me just tell you what has been going on. We didn't get the funding, which means I will continue to use my own money for the company. I want you to know that it doesn't really affect your job because we want you to stay. And I have some other news."

"Thanks for the update, but I still don't know what I am going to do in two weeks when my tourist visa has ended. And, another thing, I don't really know what my job is because I keep on getting new tasks and everything keeps on changing all the time. It's been hard to know what I'm supposed to be doing."

"Don't worry about your job. We'll figure something out, and you can choose more of what you want to work on. I apologize I haven't been able to spend much time with you or here at the office. I need to have surgery, and the doctor thinks I will be able to lead a normal life again. That is why Melinda left, and I don't want the same thing to happen to you."

"Sorry, I'm confused. Are you OK? What is going to happen to me?"

"Sierra, I thought we had some chemistry, and I'm telling you I have some health problems that only men have. By the time I have this surgery, you will come back with your visa, and we can be together."

"Uhhhh…"

"I like you, Sierra. I will give you a work visa, but you need to go back to America to finalize it anyway. When you come back, we can live together here at my apartment in Madrid."

"And your wife?"

"How did you know? Well, it doesn't matter, we are getting a divorce. I promised her that I would wait until her grandmother's affairs are settled. You know our marriage was more like a friendship the last seven years."

"Cristian, this is all a surprise to me. I needed this job, and now, finding out you are married after you made lip contact with me that one time, I feel like you deceived me. Now you want me to wait until you are divorced and have a surgery to fix your problem? For what?"

"Sierra, I don't understand you. You are single, and without me, you wouldn't have a job. Why are you being so difficult? Many women would like to be in your position. Think about what I can offer you, and let me know your decision tomorrow."

Chapter 21
Second Prize

Leaving the office after that meeting seemed like the most appropriate thing to do. I started walking somewhere, anywhere, to process the big news that had just been revealed. First, it sounded like Cristian really did like me even though he didn't act like it. But he probably didn't act like it because he was married. And the very fact that he'd brought up his failed relationship with Melinda, my competition in some regard, had me feeling like I was the second prize.

At least I was *some* prize; I reveled in that for a moment. It was first time in a long time that a guy had said he had feelings for me. I had feelings for him, though I knew my feelings could also be called delusional hallucinations that had no grounding in reality.

Second, he really did have problems. Not one but two that I knew of, and these included his body and another woman. After all, he had to be in his mid- to late forties, and it was true that those things happened to some men. Possibly the first physical misconnection we had could be related to his physical and psychological issues. But none of these things were my problem, and his lack of effort since I'd arrived here made me wonder how sincere he was.

Frankly, though, I was now able to admit to

myself that this wannabe romantic relationship between us was just a figment of my imagination. I couldn't put the blame entirely on me since his actions and behavior contributed to the confusion of my current state. The phrase he used to help convince me to take the job, "swim with the currents of life," now seemed like a concocted subliminal marketing campaign targeted at my spirit.

The phrase also could be taken to mean that if you don't swim—i.e. work and live with me— you will swim against the currents, my currents. Would something bad happen to me if I said no to his offer? Would he retaliate in some way to hurt me here in Spain? Or would I flail professionally after returning, jobless, to the U.S.?

On the other hand, I thought, maybe this was how some relationships started. There could be some obstacles to overcome that both people were willing to work out because they knew they wanted to be together. Whether they wanted to be together because they shared the same definition of love or because they had a mutual need in a complex world, it could be romantic, I guessed. And, also, it could be what was necessary for me to mature into "real adult" status with partnership responsibilities.

It had the potential to be an international love story—I could tell everyone how we'd met at a startup event in San Francisco, how we worked hard to overcome our cultural challenges to be together, how he gave me a life, including a job and a relationship. Everyone would be impressed that I learned Spanish because Madrid became my new home. And it was so exotic and amazing that two supernaturally good looking people were together.

This sounded like what my mother and everyone else wanted to repeat about me. I could hear their voices in my head: "Sierra, you finally did it. You finally got a man with money, you live with him, and you have a job. You're a 'real woman' now. No more free-spirited gallivanting around, pretending you have a career in digital marketing and escaping from your responsibilities. You can settle down now just like the rest of us boring married people who never leave the house. We are so happy for you."

Could I learn to love Cristian? Or was I just a confused millennial grasping at dollars and a dick that didn't work? It felt so wrong to even think that everyone would suddenly be happy for me if I were part of a couple, as if it was a type of achievement that merited accolades. But maybe these same judging people just say they are happy because they are like sheep—they go along with the groupthink idea that if you've got a man, a job, and some money, that is cause for some definition of happiness defined by society. But perhaps they were too confused, just like me, to really admit that maybe none of these things would make anyone happy. It was all for show anyway.

Hands down, the easiest short-term option would be to tell Cristian that I agreed to his plan of going back to the U.S. to get the work visa and coming back to live with him, probably just after his soon-to-be-ex-wife moved out. We could try out the couple life although I already knew that wouldn't work.

Another option was that I could leave him when I came back with my visa, spend more time in Madrid, and maybe find another job. Get an incredibly good-looking younger guy who doesn't speak English just to keep up appearances, mind you, and then talk about how I used an old guy to get my visa. That would be extremely risky as I had no idea how I was going to function in Madrid totally alone with my B1 Spanish level or try to have some superficial relationship. Seemed so weird.

Come on, Sierra, I told myself, *you are too jaded to try to make anything work here in Madrid after three months of floundering.* People who got second prize didn't have to take it. Even people who got first prize didn't have to take it if it wasn't right. I didn't even want to be first prize. Mentally saying no in this moment to Cristian's offer made my heart feel lighter and my spirit freer. But I was not totally convinced that this was the better option, economically speaking.

Chapter 22
April in Paris

I kept on walking and thinking, all the while dodging people who were mesmerized by their phones. On the practical side, thanks to this job, I was up to date on loan payments and even had made additional payments. I was saving money so I could take a trip and then go back to the U.S. because I knew my tourist visa was about to run out.

I went back to Mario's friend's place to eat as much as I could to stop thinking about the decision I had to make. The *aperitivo* bar's buffet was in full force with three different types of pasta, a tomato salad, and focaccia. It could have been hot dogs and fries, and I wouldn't have noticed. Binge eating was a poor excuse to remove my emotions from the situation, I knew that. It was unhealthy physically and emotionally, and I hadn't done it since that one time in high school, before applying to college, when I ate a dozen Krispy Kreme donuts and a pint of rocky road ice cream, then shoved a Whitman's Christmas Sampler by the handful into my mouth when no one was home. When they did come home, they heard me barfing for almost a half hour straight and believed it when I said I had food poisoning from bad chicken I had at the mall.

Right now, I was doing exactly what I'd said that most Americans do during the retreat from hell. At least I was mindful about it and forgetting my stupid life. Maybe I could write an article about how grateful I was to have all this food in front of me that would make me ill, and then I would be grateful I was not hungry but ill instead. What a great idea to use this opportunity: write about comparison gratitude and give thanks for being a glutton, in an op-ed piece about changing the face of millennial psychology. I had so many untapped talents; this could be a good place to start.

With food as my only friend, facing a decision as big as college choice but seeing no obvious options, I had plate after plate with my phone on the table, trying to read my horoscope to see what was around the corner of this disaster. Auspiciously, a trip was forecasted by a few astrology websites. Reading something that had been written just for me (and the billion other Virgos) felt like a special message from the universe. I believed in it because I didn't have anything else giving me some indication that I was going to be OK. None of the horoscopes said I would die. Nor did they say I was doomed to never find a job or love again. Progress was being made.

At one point, I stopped eating to glance up and saw the two bartenders looking at me. One came over, put his hand on my shoulder, and asked me, "*Cara*, are you OK?"

"Yeah, just a little hungry tonight."

"OK. Everything is going to be OK. Relax with us here for a while. Come sit at the bar."

"Thanks, but I have to get going. I have somewhere else to go."

I got up from the table slowly and felt my stomach push against the waistband of my pants. I was so bloated from the pasta and bread, the extra inches were uncomfortable. I burped as I took out my wallet and put down a five-euro bill. The bartender looked at me with sympathy in his eyes. I turned away from it immediately as I could not get emotional about the situation with Cristian or about the compassion from some strangers after they'd allowed me to decimate their buffet and burp in their faces.

As I stepped out of the restaurant, my feet directed me where to go once again. My spirit floated away somewhere. Eating had calmed me down, and my brain took a break from thinking about all that had happened just hours earlier.

I passed street after street of storefronts, restaurants, and bars. I had no idea where I was going, what I was doing, or what time it was. When I heard some drunk people speaking in English, I stopped to listen to them for a while before one saw me and said, "What are you looking at?" Then they all erupted into laughter as I turned away and started walking in the direction I just came from. My phone said 11:00 PM, and a pang of anxiety hit me. I had no clue where I was.

I looked to the window on my right and saw a funky coffee place open with a few empty tables. Without hesitation, I entered it. I took one of the empty tables all to myself and sat down to figure out the best route back to the apartment.

After I took out my phone, my ears opened to hear the slow jazz song's lyrics—"Who can I run to? What have you done to my heart?"—followed by the chorus of *April in Paris*. The sudden decision was easy: *I'll go to Paris, then fly back to Detroit.* Paris seemed like a fine place to visit from what I knew. French chocolate and wine were among my favorite things, and since I did have some discretionary income from saving, I could make it work. Besides, I needed to manifest something good before I was ready to return to Detroit to stay at my parents' home and pay them rent.

Chapter 23
Pinch Me

After making the decision to go to Paris, I got a tea and watched people in the café. Even though it was almost 1:00 AM, I felt a lot safer being out in Madrid than other cities. I finished my tea and headed to the metro with the help of Google Maps. The metro was still running and a bit crowded with a variety of people, from senior citizens to high schoolers out and about on a Friday night. Even though a good number were inebriated and I was annoyed by their behavior, which included singing and making out, I wasn't afraid of crazy people doing crazy things like in San Francisco.

Safely home, I quickly did my bedtime routine and then looked for a way to get to Paris on my laptop. The excitement I felt outweighed my anxiety about money and my career. Airfare seemed kind of pricey for a one-way, last-minute flight. I wasn't ready to buy a ticket just yet. I wondered whether I could take a train there because that might be more fun and probably cheaper. I decided I would sleep on it and buy a ticket tomorrow. It would be a lot easier to tell Cristian I was not interested in his offer on Monday if I had a ticket and could say, "I'm going to Paris." Anyway, it sounded and felt better than saying, "I'm going back to Detroit." I had no idea what I was really doing, but I had a feeling Paris would be the most fun, a little extravagant, and not dull.

I closed my laptop and put it under my bed. I was so happy thinking about this trip. I closed my eyes, smiling and envisioning the Eiffel Tower, sidewalk cafés, and French waiters. Paris would be so amazing.

Drifting off into sleep was effortless. I woke up Saturday afternoon at 2:00 PM feeling like a different person and in the same good mood that I went to bed with. But as I lay in bed, my dream was coming back to me.

The dream started off with me being lost in an office with cubicles and people all around me. It was noisy and a bit chaotic. What I was supposed to be doing there, I hadn't a clue now, nor did I in the dream. Then I realized I was in the middle of the floor and started walking around when a man with a bike came up to me and said, "Follow me." I didn't question why the guy had his bike with him in the office, and I ended up following him until we left the office. While I didn't remember what the guy looked like, he was nice and showed up right in the middle of my struggling to find my way.

Despite the brevity of my recollection of the dream, it left me with a warm feeling that somehow I would find my way. I did not put too much stock in the fact that it was a man who showed me the way because Cristian, the yoga retreat leader, and my old boss, Bob Martinez from Brown and White, had turned me more cynical about older men.

I realized, in analyzing this dream, that there was no way that I could take the next step by myself. And, while I'd had more than my friends' share of drama, I held on to what the dream meant to me: I would find my way with the help of a kind soul.

Chapter 24
Closure

I prepared myself Monday morning before work by sitting down and thinking about what I was going to say to Cristian. With the three sentences written down, I held them in my hand, memorizing them on my walk to work. I wanted to be clear that I was quitting today and that I was going to Paris. I would say these lines in an authoritative tone and think about when he called me an intern to get the courage to demand the respect I deserved. I would also be neutral and not think about the strange Spanish kiss or how it was nice not to pay rent for three months.

For a change, when I arrived at 9:30 AM, the office seemed crowded. Alex and Fernando were meeting with Cristian in the one conference room that had a window. I waved as I walked by while they just briefly nodded.

My desk had an envelope on it with my name on the outside. The envelope was from Cristian's other company. I opened the letter to find a job offer in Spanish and a sticky note that said, "Take this when you apply for your visa at the Spanish Consulate." It was outlining some details that I guessed were required.

On some level, Cristian had just showed he really did mean what he said. He was serious about helping me get the visa and working for him. I wasn't prepared for this. The love part I wasn't so sure of; there was no love letter in the envelope. Only the job offer with the note.

Confused, I sat down and held the offer letter in my hand. I closed my eyes and turned toward the window. If anyone was walking by, they wouldn't see that my eyes were closed. Was this love? Was this my career break? I wanted to think of something wise to reassure me. I couldn't.

I kept my eyes closed. I checked out and went somewhere deep in my mind until I remembered the dream. When I'd woken up this morning, I'd known Cristian wasn't the man, but I could have been wrong. Was Cristian really the one to guide me through the next phase?

After some time, I opened my eyes and took out my computer. Cristian had sent me a meeting invite for 11:00 AM. I RSVP'ed "maybe" but then changed it to "yes." Why I chose "maybe" in the first place, I wasn't too sure. Everything had been a "maybe" since I got here. "Maybe" this would work out. "Maybe" Cristian would be my boyfriend. "Maybe" I would make enough money to stay. "Maybe" the startup would do well.

It was time for the wishy-washy "maybe" phase to end. I started deleting emails, trashed old documents in the share drive, and cleaned out my download folder. My mind was made up. The letter didn't change my intuition. I needed to trust myself.

At 11:00 AM, I went to Cristian's office, but he

was not there. I stood outside the door with my arms crossed for a few minutes. I didn't know how long I should wait, but I realized it looked a bit strange to have someone waiting outside an empty office. For the next few minutes, on the way to my desk, I wondered why he'd set up that meeting time and then hadn't shown up. This was the first time that he had scheduled a meeting with me and then stood me up. I wanted to tell him my memorized three lines and then leave. But by him not showing up, more anxiety was building, and the second thoughts were multiplying.

Once I was at my desk, I immediately bought my train ticket to Paris to leave in one week. This was the necessary step I had to make to stop thinking about accepting the job offer. I thought traveling by train from Madrid to Paris with connections in Barcelona and Narbonne would allow me to see more.

I also was excited that I wouldn't have to pay a fee for my suitcases, like on a plane. I wondered whether I could check my luggage the same way you did on a plane or whether I'd end up storing them somewhere. I'd taken Amtrak once before, from D.C. to New York, but I didn't have two big suitcases then to worry about.

The rest of the day, I didn't see or hear from Cristian. At 5:30 PM, I decided to write my three lines in an email.

Dear Cristian:

Thank you for this opportunity. April 15 will be my last day here. I will vacate the apartment on April 16 to go to Paris.

Sincerely,

Sierra

The moment I sent that email, I felt empowered. I finally felt like I was on the right track, even though this track had no real trajectory or incoming cash flow. I reminded myself that I deserved this break.

The next day, Cristian replied to my email with "OK. Leave the keys on the table. Send me your last invoice before you go. Wish you the best." The email was signed off with only his appended signature. The cold and curt email bothered me for a moment. But then I realized the roller coaster of the past few months was now over.

I knew I should have given two weeks' notice to ParaLlevar, but it seemed like it didn't matter to Cristian. It also seemed not to matter to him that we wouldn't say goodbye or wrap up the job in person. I felt that if he really did care about me, he wouldn't act like this, so that reaffirmed my decision to move ahead. It was probably for the best that this was over quickly.

This freedom that I was about to enjoy was the result of the struggle of the past few years. Now it was really time to celebrate Sierra, instead of always being in one fight or the other—Sierra vs.

Sierra, Sierra vs. jobs, Sierra vs. Madrid. Going on a vacation by myself was something I had never done before, so why not take advantage of being in Europe and go to Paris?

I wondered whether this was what retirement would feel like, knowing that you didn't have to go back to the office and could have all the time in the world to do whatever you wanted, just like those people on the English vacation. You just couldn't spend a lot of money because you didn't really have a lot of money.

But I didn't know when I would tell my parents I was going back to stay with them in Detroit. I also wanted to avoid telling them that I had quit the job. And, as far as the dreamt-up romantic scenario with Cristian and his offer to sponsor my visa went, that was better left to a movie I wanted to make someday. From his wife to his illness to the job offer, it felt like one of those *telenovelas* I'd recently started to watch. While many times I did not understand all of the Spanish, I could tell that most of the plots were pure dysfunction that I didn't think could happen until I got to Madrid.

I thought it was a non-issue that I was going to stay a few weeks past the ninety-day tourist visa. I heard many Americans did it. If there was a problem, I would solve it when it would happen. I was tired of worrying anyway.

Chapter 25
Riding the Rails

On this fresh spring morning, the smell of fragrant blooming flowers mixed with car exhaust permeated the air during my walk to Atocha train station. It wasn't a far walk from the apartment, and I thought it would be good to save a few euros and get some exercise before my long ten-hour journey to Paris. With me, I had my two suitcases and my backpack that was stuffed with snacks from Mercadona: almonds, chips, apples, and a California salad. I also had a few packs of tissue and antibacterial gel to get me through the punishment of public toilets.

By the time I got to Atocha train station, I was drenched in sweat and smelled like I just came from working out. I knew I didn't have time to change but thought I could cool off once inside. But inside it felt like the jungle on a summer day, owing its humidity to the indoor planetarium of ponds and palm trees.

Despite my sweatiness, I wanted to enjoy this indoor garden atmosphere, but my train was going to leave in about twenty minutes, and there was no way I was going to miss that. I pushed my luggage to the platform and waited until the agent would allow people on board. There already was a crowd gathering of maybe forty Indian people near the platform getting ready to board.

"Buenos días. ¿Hablas inglés?" escaped from my mouth. Too late, I realized I should have used

the formal instead of the informal to address the uniformed woman on the train. I was pushing one suitcase in front and dragging the other from behind in the narrow corridor.

"Yes. A little," she replied, looking worriedly at my luggage.

"I'm looking for my seat," I said and handed her my ticket. Already exhausted from the journey— which technically hadn't even started yet—I stopped pushing my suitcases.

"Your bags won't fit in the car, miss."

"OK, but where is my seat?"

"I'll take your bags and put them over here. You will have to buy another ticket just for your bags."

Confused and annoyed that I might have to pay for another seat, I defensively spoke up: "The website didn't say there was a limit on luggage. I just want to find my seat, and then we can talk about my suitcases."

"Miss, you have to pay. Your seat is right over there, in this compartment. But your bags won't fit there. You have to pay since your bags are like another person."

Turned out my seat was actually in a compartment of four fold-down beds and a sink. The carlike cabin already had three women sitting inside who glared at me when I entered, leaving my bags in the corridor. "*Hola*," I said with a fake smile, trying to be friendly. It was a real struggle to force myself to be friendly when I had zero personal space. And it was true: There was no way my bags and my body could fit here.

After a few minutes of me sitting down and then standing up and trying to shove one bag under a seat, the same train agent reappeared and said, "Miss, come here."

Pushing my bags again through the corridor and then into an entirely new train car, we passed Indians who were smoking out the windows already, and the train hadn't even left the station yet. "*No fumar*. No smoking," she yelled at them, but, she didn't tell them *they* had to pay. I wondered whether I was following her to go pay somewhere on the train.

Then, we entered another car that had noticeably fewer people. I only saw a man standing at the door to his compartment. Overall, this train car was a lot cleaner, cooler, and quieter. The agent pointed to a luggage area and said, "Miss, you can put your bags here, and take a seat in this compartment."

I put my bags in the luggage area that was next to my new compartment. It didn't look that secure, but I highly doubted that someone would take my bags because Madrid and Europe in general just seemed so much safer than any U.S. city I'd been to. I would try to keep an eye out when I could since my laptop was inside one of the bags.

"*Gracias*," I said to the woman, but she had already turned to leave the train car.

Chapter 26
Breakdown

"*Hola*," said a blonde-haired, chipper-looking Anglophone college student. "What's your name?"

I glanced down to see her TOMS shoes were on the floor next to her seat and that her toenails were painted baby blue. "Sierra. Pleased to meet you. What's your name?"

"Lizzie. I'm from Toronto. Where are you from, and what are you doing in Spain?"

"I'm from Detroit, and I had a job in Madrid for a few months. Now I'm going to Paris on a little vacation. And you?"

"Oh, I was doing a semester abroad in Madrid. And now I'm going to Barcelona to meet my boyfriend's family and friends. Hey, did you see all those Indians on this train?"

"Yes, I noticed the Indians." I was wondering where this was going.

"You know, it's kinda fun to pretend we are poor like them and ride a train instead of fly. I've never ridden a train before, but my boyfriend told me I had to do it. I don't know what all these Indians are doing here in Europe. But you know, it *is* the EU, and you can go anywhere and do anything here once you are in."

I was afraid this boyfriend would be number three in the compartment. "Is your boyfriend going to be joining us?" I asked and then looked toward my backpack, which I grabbed nervously, ready to bolt.

"Oh, no, he is already in Barcelona. He's going to be waiting for me at the train station in Barcelona. Then we're supposed to go to a hotel because we can't really have sex in his parents' house, he said. I guess they are like ultraconservative or something. I hope they like me because I want to marry him." And with that she took out her phone, held it up to the practiced best photogenic angle possible, and took not one but three selfies.

"Sounds fun," I said, getting up with my backpack, now bolting out of the compartment. Being reminded of what life was like for most of the people in my age bracket was not what I needed at this moment. I could have lied and said I had a boyfriend who was super rich and good looking who was waiting for me, too. He even wanted me to live with him, after his wife moved out.

I thought I'd be brave and take a walk to meet the Indians. I could probably find one who wanted to have a conversation in English with me, and heck, maybe one would want to get married, too. I would charge $10,000 because I knew it wouldn't be for love but a visa, and with that money I could make a bigger dent in my loans. I knew that was a lot, but I'd once seen a Craigslist post that offered that compensation for being a visa bride, so that could be an option for me one day if I needed money and someone to take home to Detroit.

I walked through the train cars but didn't stop. I looked in the train compartments to see all the Indians together, laughing and smiling in their collectivist culture impromptu groups. Some were playing cards; others were talking. No one was looking for an outsider to talk to, let alone marry.

My wandering continued. There had to be someone here that wanted to talk to me because I wanted to talk to someone. I got to the café car and sat down at an empty table. I would test the law of attraction; by sitting there all alone, I would then attract some quality people to talk to me. Smiling as people walked by, I was more than secretly hoping someone would sit down on their own, or that it would get too crowded and they wouldn't have a choice.

"There you are! I thought I lost you. You want a *café con leche*?" said happy Lizzie.

"No, thanks," I replied with a grimace.

Chapter 27
Transfer

Lizzie had a mouth on her that showed no signs of closing anytime soon. I imagined that she must have been nervous about meeting her boyfriend's family and friends. But she probably had a dependent personality that was, in a word, annoying. I wondered whether she'd gotten bored with taking selfies in the train compartment and then came to look for me.

She continued talking about her school and how she'd partied and cavorted around Madrid like a crazy repressed college student on a perpetual spring break (which she basically was). Then she yammered about how she'd met Juan and that changed everything and there were so many things that they were planning on doing in Barcelona.

I politely smiled, blocked out her words, and looked out the window. Dotted with an occasional tree or small farm, the landscape was mostly a boring continuation of one-dimension flatness. Kind of like Lizzie. It also looked very dry. There were a few small-town train stations that we sped by but not many.

I wished the train could magically find a place where it was perfect for me and I didn't have to struggle so much and just drop me off there. I didn't care how long it took, as hellish as the forced social interaction was, as long as the train stopped at exactly the right time for me. I wished that I had more time on the train to think and be away from everything. The world was so confusing, and being here in Europe didn't help me get a clear picture of what I was going to do next. On the train, I felt safe and disconnected with no pressure to do anything. I now could understand a little bit why homeless people would ride buses and subways all day.

After an hour in the café car, I excused myself and made my way back to our compartment to take a nap. Lizzie said she wasn't tired and would not bother me, which was kind of her. I was able to take a rest, and when I woke up, a garbled announcement was being made and the train was starting to slow down.

Within twenty minutes, the train would be arriving at Barcelona Sants train station. Everyone would have to get off. I would have to make a transfer there, and then I still had to go to Narbonne and Toulouse before I made it to Paris.

I went to get my suitcases and push them to the door. Getting off the train was impossible by myself, but some nice man helped me get both suitcases out of the train and onto the platform. I rolled them both into the station to see which platform my next train would leave from. With two more transfers still to come, I now understood why this ticket had been so cheap. After getting the platform number, I walked back out to the platform area to wait until boarding began.

Looking around, I saw that this train was going to be crowded. When the train started boarding, no one cared about my luggage or told me I had to pay more for it, but I couldn't find a place to store it near my seat. This leg of the trip was only an hour and a half, so I figured it was going to be fine if I put my bags in another car that had luggage space but no seats and took a seat in a car that had seats but no space.

The train left Barcelona on time and made it to Narbonne, France, ahead of schedule. People were pushing to get off, and I had to wait to go to the other car to get my suitcases. I knew exactly where I left them, so naturally I began to panic when I discovered that they were not there. *Maybe someone moved them*, I thought. I saw an agent, but he said they hadn't moved any bags. I walked through every car on the train, looking high and low for my suitcases. No luck. They were gone.

Chapter 28
Surreality

Remarkably calm, I got off the train with only my backpack and headed into Narbonne's train station. My phone would turn on, but I was not able to make any calls. Walking around the station for a few minutes, I finally found a kiosk with a guy who spoke English to help me buy a French SIM card and install it in my phone.

But once my phone was working again, I didn't know who to call or what website to look up to help me. I did a few more circles around the train station with my phone in my hand to think of what to do. Fully immersed in problem-solving mode, I still wasn't actually processing that all my stuff had been stolen, although it did feel really good not to have to lug around two suitcases.

I went back to the English-speaking guy and asked him what I should do. He said to go to the ticketing desk inside the station and file a report, which was exactly the guidance I needed to stop walking aimlessly around and do something about my situation.

"Hi, all my stuff was stolen off the train from Barcelona to here," I said in a rather calm way to the ticketing agent.

"Miss, do you have any proof?" said the uptight man who must have spent hours perfecting his uniformed look and perfectly coiffed hair.

"Yes, I have proof. I don't have anything with me. Someone stole my stuff. My computer is in there. It's all gone!" By then, it hit me: I was now shit out of luck in France, with nothing but some snacks, tissues, my wallet, passport, and phone. Thank God I had at least that.

"We do not take responsibility for lost or stolen items. That is on our website and on your ticket. You should have watched your bags during your trip. And, since you got off the train and missed your transfer, you will not make it to Paris tonight."

"What?" I was so confused and upset, my right hand shot up in the air and then landed in a fist on the counter.

"Miss, I can reissue a ticket at no charge to get you to Paris tomorrow. But I cannot help you with your bags. They are gone."

"I'm going to call the police. Then I'm going to tell the consulate. This is not right. All my things were stolen. Do you know that I am an American? We do what is right!" I sounded like a politician.

"Hello, pretty woman," a voice from behind me said in a Spanish accent.

"Oh stop with the fake compliments, dammit. Why are you calling my ass pretty? I don't want to help you with your fucking English." I was livid as I turned around to see a very handsome black man wearing a fitted T-shirt showing off his abs of steel, standing with a bike.

"Give me one moment and we'll go have a coffee. Don't worry," he said calmly as he went to the counter and spoke in French. The man from the counter left and came back with a large box, which Mr. Abs loaded on the back of his bike as if it weighed nothing.

I sullenly stared at him and wondered what his next pickup line would be. Then I questioned why I was even going for a coffee with some player who called me the lamest name from a movie ever. *This guy is ridiculous and trying to pretend he is smooth so he can take advantage of me having a low travel moment*, I told myself. I clutched my backpack and then moved it to the front of my body like a fake baby.

Mr. Abs gave me a smile and said, "Let's go!" He walked with his bike, and I walked alongside. He seemed cheerful and had a nice smile that he wasn't afraid to show. Still, I thought, *they are all the same, these men who want to learn English and be "friends" with Americans.*

We went to a small café just outside the train station, and he parked his bike near the table. He ordered two espressos for us in French, and they came within seconds. I think he could tell something was wrong. I really didn't know whether I could trust this man or not. He was kind enough not to start asking me questions but just smiled and seemed to be waiting for me to say something.

"Hi. Thanks for this coffee. But you know, I don't like coffee," I said in a snotty way as if coffee were some horrible beverage and I needed something better.

"It's OK. I'll drink yours. What would you like?"

"A tea, please."

With that, he called over the server, and a tea came within minutes.

"I'm Ismael. I'm from Cuba. I know my English is not that good. I saw you had a problem, and I wanted to help you. Even though it's a small town, you can get lost here. Are you OK?"

I had never met a black person who spoke Spanish or anyone from Cuba, for that matter. He also spoke French, and his English was very good. Since I didn't have much to be stolen now, or much to lose, I decided to open up to him. He made eye contact and seemed sincere enough to make sure at least I got my beverage of choice.

"I'm sorry if I wasn't polite to you. I'm Sierra. I'm American, from Detroit. All my stuff got stolen on that train, and I'm stuck here tonight before I can go to Paris." Then, like a brilliant flash of lightning, my dream came back to me: a man with a bike walking with me and helping me. It was already predestined that I would meet this man.

"Don't worry. Travelers like you from all over the world have come. You can stay with me for free if you want, and you can help around my place. You know, a 'work/trade.' Our possessions possess us sometimes. The good thing is that you are safe, healthy, and beautiful. *Hay que sonreír a la vida.*"

"You are the guy from my dream," I said, looking at him and then his bike.

"Tell me the story another time. Sounds interesting. We'll have to get going if you want to come."

"Yes, OK," I said, putting my faith in the universe that this was all happening as it should.

Chapter 29
A Free Place to Stay

Ismael looked at my backpack and then gently took it from me. He put it on his shoulders and started walking his bike. The box was on the back of the bike, and Ismael looked like he had everything under control. He was most definitely in super good shape. Not an ounce of fat on him. I wondered how many hours a day he worked out to look like a professional athlete.

"Sierra, are you OK to walk about thirty minutes to my place? I will tell you more about where I live."

"Sure, that's fine. I will remember the way because I have to come back tomorrow to get the train to Paris. Thirty minutes is not that much," I said and gave him a sincere smile.

"That is a good idea. Where I live, there are a few houses together, and I have a big house. I came from Cuba fifteen years ago, and, well, it's a long story how I ended up here. But the house is mine now, and I share it with those that need a home."

I was imagining that this was going to be like a secret hostel with really cool people from all over the world. I was betting there would be at least a few surfers from Australia and maybe a sarcastic English girl and some crazy Japanese students. The odds of one person there being single, who could then be my friend, had to be good. I just hoped there were no bedbugs.

But what if there was a hidden trick here? Maybe I needed to get a little bit smarter and have more street smarts about me. I'd just gotten my stuff stolen because I wasn't paying attention. Now, I needed to stay alert. I needed to ask what Ismael really meant about people who needed a home. It could be a homeless shelter or a brothel or some crack house.

"You know, I don't do drugs," I said, then followed up with, "How many people live there with you?" A not-so-brilliantly subtle way to find out whether he really was into something shady, although what would I even do now that he had my backpack?

"It depends. Sometimes I have a mix of travelers, boys, girls, men, and women. Some people stay with me for five, six years. A good home can be hard to find. We take care of animals, too. Do you like animals?"

"Very much so," I said. I couldn't stop thinking, *it is just like my dream; he is walking with me and has a bike.*

"Great. You can feed the chickens tonight," he said with a chuckle. We walked on, talking occasionally about Narbonne and the train to Paris. I was not revealing any personal information until I saw what kind of place he had.

As we turned a corner, Ismael said his house was the blue one about twenty feet ahead. The gravel street made a crunchy noise that filled our conversation gaps until we got closer to the house. The pale blue house looked to have two floors and an attic with four windows. It was rather large and probably had more than six bedrooms, I estimated. A mob of kids ran up to greet us when we got to the driveway. They hugged Ismael's legs first, then some came over to give me a little hug or touch on the leg.

"Are these kids yours?" I asked bluntly.

"They are as long as they stay here. Sierra, this place is an orphanage and animal shelter for this town. I take care of the people that don't have a place to go, and most of them are kids. It's part of my life path. Sometimes travelers like you come and help me out. You are welcome to stay tonight with us, but if you don't like kids, then there is a hotel back near the train station," Ismael said in an earnest way.

"It's fine. I like kids. I get it," I said, unsure of myself and the unfamiliar situation. A man who took care of kids and animals and put more emphasis on other people's well-being than his own was new to me. His values seemed to be centered on the well-being of others, namely children and animals. If he really was the man from my dream, and he was sincere in helping me at least for tonight and all these kids and animals, then why I was acting like I wanted there to be some big drama that was going to explode like everything else in my life? I complained when things didn't go right, but when things did go right, like now, there was no need to expect the worst.

Chapter 30
Shorfanage

Ismael parked his bike, lifted the box, and pushed the front door open to let the kids and myself inside. The kids rushed into the living room, where there were two girls who looked to be about fourteen watching TV. They greeted Ismael with a "Bonjour," and then Ismael walked back to the kitchen. It smelled like a pot roast was cooking, reminding me that I hadn't eaten since I was on the train.

In the kitchen, there was a portly, older, dark-skinned woman who started speaking to Ismael in Spanish, but it was so fast I couldn't understand anything. She looked at me, smiled, and said, much slower, "Welcome, lady."

"I'm the only one who speaks English here, at least enough to have a conversation. This is Rosa, and she is from the Dominican Republic. She's been helping me three days a week to cook and clean. We have ten kids now living here full time until someone adopts them or their parents come back. We have some cats that come and go, three dogs, a goat, and chickens in the back."

The dogs started barking, the kids were talking loudly about something, and the TV volume seemed to be too loud for anyone to have a conversation. This place was a zoo. I was wondering how many kids would be in my room. *It's just for one night, you can manage*, I told myself. *And don't forget, you are going to Paris tomorrow. Rough it on this orphan farm for one night, and then go eat chocolate and drink champagne until you can't walk anymore.*

"Can I see the goat?" I asked inquisitively. "I'm a goat in Chinese astrology, but I've never seen one."

"Sure, you can go out and feed the chickens and the goat. There is some food in the back in the plastic container. There's one for the chickens and one for the goat. You'll see it out there."

In the backyard, I saw the goat, who looked about as old as I was. "Poor old French goat," I said. It gently lifted its head to meet my hand and then let out a funny noise. I put my cheek on the top of the goat's head. I finally understood that this place really was an orphanage and an animal shelter, taking in people and animals that had nowhere to go. Both the orphans and animals were taking care of each other here at the shorfanage, in one artificially created family setting. Then I heard some feet come up behind me.

"Hi hi hi," said a boy of about five who could have passed for possessed. His thick, curly blond hair was out of control. He started laughing loudly as he ran away from me toward the chickens, trying to catch them.

I almost forgot it was my assigned task to feed them. I walked over to grab the plastic container. Then I went over to the boy and motioned to him to grab some food. He then started laughing again as he took two fistfuls of the grain and threw it up to the sky, pelting some chickens who were slow to run away. The boy then took off into the house, laughing all the way. I went back to the old goat, found its food nearby, and put a handful in a bowl near the fence.

After my feeding duties were over, I returned to the house to find the two large tables in the kitchen and back room being set for dinner. I wanted a few moments to myself before dinner and asked Rosa where Ismael was. She pointed upstairs, and I walked upstairs, calling "Ismael?"

He was in one room making a bed. "Hi, Sierra, you sleep here in this room. Here are some old sweats you can use for pajamas. We're going to eat dinner in about twenty minutes."

"Is this your room?" I asked after noticing a big Cuban flag and some picture frames.

"It's your room tonight."

"Thank you, Ismael. I'll be down for dinner, and I can help clean up, too." I could see he looked tired and a little sad.

He smiled and then left the room, closing the door behind him. My backpack was on a chair near the door with a fresh folded towel next to it. I looked at the pictures and saw some were of kids while others were of a whole family. One kid I could see was Ismael and what had to be his sister at the beach laughing on a towel. I wondered how old he was because the pictures looked like they were from the '80s and he was at least ten then.

My plan was to get in a short power nap before dinner, so I didn't pull back the sheets and get too comfortable. I closed my eyes, and when I woke, I looked at my phone to see that it was now ten o'clock. I scrambled downstairs to find Rosa cleaning up the kitchen and Ismael sitting at the table with some papers.

"*Pobrecita*," she said in a caring way.

"Sorry, Ismael. I wanted to help, but I fell asleep."

"It's OK, Sierra. We made you a plate of food. It's over there," he said in a friendly way.

I took the plate of food and sat down across from Ismael. I ate in silence, watching Ismael work on paying bills or doing something. I knew it wasn't polite to ask questions, especially since I said I was going to help and then fell asleep—which may have been why Ismael was also not speaking to me.

"Tomorrow, Sierra, you need to leave for the train station an hour early to give you enough time. Maybe one of the kids will want to walk with you there. Some of them know a few words in English. You can teach them a few more words on the way."

"OK, sounds good. Thank you for everything, Ismael. It was really nice of you to help me earlier today and offer me your bed. I mean, I should say

I'm sorry, too, for not being nice to you before. I've never met anyone like you or seen a place like this. Most people I meet are so worried about impressing other people with superficial things. Myself included. I'm caught up in trying to get a job to pay my loans, not get fat, and not have breakouts, and I'm always looking for a boyfriend. But things never go how I want them to. Life is more than these stupid things when your stuff gets stolen, you don't speak the language, and have nowhere to sleep."

"Sierra, I'm writing down what you have said to remind you of it when you get caught up in yourself again," Ismael said, chuckling, and then he really was writing something down. "You know in Cuba, we say *no hay precio más que una vida*, which means there is no price more than a human life. I believe this, and that is why I am happy here. One day, you'll find the meaning to your life."

Chapter 31
Hard Choices

Before I changed into the sweats that would be my pajamas and got ready for bed, I sat down and looked again at the pictures in his room. Ismael defied all male archetypes and seemed to operate from a place of selflessness. He wasn't trying to prove anything, yet he was a stand-up example of human kindness. His faith that everything was going to work out just fine inspired trust in me. This made him different from other men, and women, who had cycled through my life. He had the right and perfect job for him, and he knew it was his life path. I wondered whether that made it easier for him to be such a good guy. I wished I knew what I was supposed to do and how to find my life path instead of obsessing over stupid things.

The modern values of consumerism and accumulation, narcissism and superficiality, and independence and manipulation were absent here. No one was running around addicted to their phone or was wearing headphones and fancy designer clothes. My mind went in reverse to remember the events of the day and that I had lost two suitcases filled with my stuff. Someone somewhere maybe was wearing my dirty clothes and trying to use my laptop. But really, the events of the past twenty-four hours seemed so trivial when I started thinking about kids who didn't have a home.

After sleeping the night and eating breakfast, which consisted of a piece of baguette with butter on it, my time was up here. I took my backpack, gave Ismael a hug, and said thank you again. Rosa, who by chance was going to the center in her car, gave me a ride to the train station. I thanked her and got out. I turned to wave, watching the car drive away.

I went up to the ticket counter to find the same agent, who was again perfectly coiffed, and asked for my ticket to be refunded. Surprisingly, he refunded my credit card without any hassle. I then asked whether there was a package for Ismael and he said yes, there was another one from yesterday that he hadn't picked up yet. I bet that Ismael would be coming back today for it, so I decided to wait for him. If he didn't show up, then I would do something else, I just didn't know what.

At around one, I saw Ismael riding his bike, then dismounting to walk his bike into the train station.

"Ismael," I said, waving.

"Pretty woman, what happened? You missed your train?"

"No, I missed my life. I mean, I don't have a life. A real one. And, I'm not an adult, either. I want to stay at your place. Take care of the kids and the goat. Find some meaning in something. You know, when you have nothing, you can risk everything."

"I'm sure we can work something out. But it's not easy, and my life is a lot different than your American life. You might get bored with how we live," he said stoically.

"I'm not happy with my American life. And there are a lot of things I need to learn. I've always believed that your feelings are never wrong. I feel lost in my life, and traveling has been a distraction from myself, but I'm lonely and don't know who I am or who I'd like to be. I keep on comparing myself to other people and wonder why I don't have what they have. Madrid was a complete disaster and I, and I—" And with that, I started to cry. Ismael came over and put his arm around my shoulder. "—and I don't want to go back to the U.S. because I have nothing and I am nothing."

"Sierra, we all feel like orphans sometimes. We'll go back and plan out a week for you to help and teach English a few hours, if you want. I'll also see if we have some clothes for you to wear, or we'll go to Kiabi if you need something," Ismael said, like he heard a dramatic speech like mine a hundred times a day. "And, Sierra, you are someone."

Chapter 32
English Lessons

Ismael picked up the second box and put it on the back of his bike just like yesterday. His demeanor was the same, even and steady, as he told me that the box had come from a church that gave them clothes and sheets from time to time. My mind was now adjusting to a lifestyle that was a lot slower and focused on the day-to-day tasks of living.

The conversation flowed, and Ismael told me a little bit more about Narbonne. As I noticed, not all of the children were French; some came with their moms and dads, who were seasonal workers. Some kids just stayed during the tourist season. It seemed like a very flexible situation, and all the children went to the local school.

When we got to the house, there were two boys who looked to be brothers of about eight or ten sitting down on the step to the door. One had an envelope that he gave to Ismael, and they spoke in French. Ismael opened the door, and the two brothers went in. "We will make room for these brothers from Sierra Leone."

"Are you ever worried that you won't have enough room for these kids? Or enough food? I don't want to be in the way. Maybe I should go," I worriedly said.

"Sometimes we have to get creative. If you want to leave at any time, you know you don't have any obligations to me," he said, followed by, "I was going to ask you to clean the garage out. We have some tables and a chalkboard there. There are some books, and maybe some are in English. You will have your first class with these two new arrivals in one hour, then after the kids come home, you'll have another class. Sound good?

"But I'm not a teacher. How do I know what to do?" I asked.

"You know more than these students. I think you'll be fine."

I walked out to the garage to find a pretty decent classroom. The garage also had a few windows high near the ceiling, which allowed for some natural light. Overall, it was on the small side but clean and had three tables with four chairs at each table. There was a bookshelf in the back with a bunch of school-books and some random comics and storybooks. In the front, there was a chalkboard on wheels and some chalk. I saw a rag and wiped off the tables. I then put some paper and pencils at two places.

The brothers came in and took their seats at the places with the paper and pencils. I started by teaching them the alphabet song, then read them a book. They were very well behaved and didn't say much. I imagined they must also have been confused and scared, and I wanted to hug them after class, but I didn't think that was appropriate for a teacher to do. After their class was finished, I sat down and looked at more books and tried to remember some more songs. The second group of kids came in, and I started again.

By the time the second group was finished, I was tired. I walked back into the house to see Ismael cooking dinner. *It must be Rosa's day off*, I thought. I volunteered to help, and he gave me the potatoes to peel.

Ismael took a seat opposite me at the table and started peeling carrots. "How did the English classes go?"

"Good, considering I have no experience teaching English. Except for that program I did back a few weeks ago in Alicante where I had to speak in English with a Spanish speaker for one week. That was a bit stressful at times because there was a cultural and language difference. I think these kids are more fun," I said with a smile.

"You didn't get along with Spanish people?" Ismael looked at me and raised an eyebrow.

"No, not really. I thought I was going to have a job and maybe a boyfriend there, but nothing worked out, and turned out he was married and had some other problems. Physical and mental, I mean," I said in a nervous way. That was totally too much information that I just shared and made me look like an amateur psychologist.

"Well, you know Spain is different. And you know what they say about Spanish people and sex, don't you?" Ismael gave me another look, with both eyebrows raised this time.

"No. I wasn't able to find out," I said candidly.

"Hahaha. That is funny. Spanish men are not like real Latin lovers, and sounds like you found out enough to know there wasn't anything worth your while there. But why were you going to Paris?"

"Oh, it doesn't matter now. I think I'll stay a few weeks here, if that is OK?"

"As long as you like, Sierra," Ismael said with a smile.

Chapter 33
Karma

I had given up on romance after I left Madrid and wasn't looking for something romantic in Ismael, but the more I got to know him, the more fun we had. Discovering Ismael and I were very compatible didn't take long, and within a week after I arrived, we started a romantic relationship. There was some truth behind the sensual and sensitive Latin lover stereotype. Ismael was warm and caring, in addition to being emotionally and physically available. Many women would have agreed that he also was easy on the eyes as my sassy grandmother would say.

I didn't care that he was black or from Cuba. But I knew what my parents and extended family thought about interracial relationships, which differed depending on the situation. In public, with non-family members around, my family had no problem with people from different races being involved with each other. However, at family dinners it was a different story, and one time when I was home on spring break during my freshman year, my Mom said out of the blue that I was not to date black men ever and if I did, I would have to face the consequences.

Whatever those consequences were, I had no idea, nor did I give a rat's ass the older I got. It felt like my life was moving at warp speed, kind of like dog years, where I skipped ahead to my forties thanks to the past few years of stress related to finding a career, having financial responsibilities, and going through romantic catastrophes.

I was fed up with society, and Ismael was showing me something I couldn't pass up. Reflecting further on my decision to become involved with Ismael, I realized he was the complete opposite of impotent and indecisive Cristian. That led to me to worry that Ismael could be considered a rebound. But I thought it through and assured myself that Ismael wasn't a rebound, since there was no guy in the first place to rebound from, only an emotional and professional mess in Madrid.

Stepping into the role of English teacher and nanny, I didn't mind taking care of the kids and helping out around the shorfanage. They were a good group, with some occasional behavioral problems that didn't amount to any real stress on my part. This was the first time that I'd had such a big responsibility in making sure everyone was fine, was fed, and didn't blow up anything—and I wasn't even getting paid.

One night, after dinner, Ismael seemed to be more serious than usual. The children cleaned the table and put away the leftovers, then went to their rooms or to the living room to watch TV. Ismael and I were sitting at the table with the chore calendar when he asked me, "Do you think there is more racism in the U.S., Spain, or France?

"I think racism is different everywhere you go. In my own life, people have thought I was part black and have openly asked me if I was black or Hispanic during job interviews. And in Spain, I only saw black people begging outside supermarkets or in the park selling things. I didn't really ask people about racism in Madrid, though," I said thoughtfully.

"Interesting. I heard Spain has a lot of racism, but I have only experience in France."

"Seems like the kids get along just fine and they are all pretty diverse."

"Do you think because of the way you look and because you're American, you have more freedom to do what you want?"

"I kind of get what you're asking, I think. But I don't understand the freedom part. Up until now, I've been fighting to be part of the status quo—you know, get a degree, look for a job, move up in society. I just took the job in Madrid because I didn't have a job in the U.S. Part of me is angry that I can't fit in and be normal. And, since I'm ethnically ambiguous, people get confused, which doesn't mean I have more freedom, just more people asking me questions and trying to figure me out."

"Are your ethnically ambiguous parents supportive? Do they want you to work or to settle down?" observed Ismael, making intense eye contact. Maybe since our relationship could get more serious, he was trying to figure out whether

I was capable of the long term. I was sensing this conversation had been on his mind for some time and was important to him.

"I haven't talked to them much since I've been in Europe. They have no clue about how hard it is to get a job these days. And, I don't think they are happy that I'm single. But the truth is, I don't know how to settle down," I said and then got up from the table.

I was unable to deal with my emotions. This was not the same culture-shock feeling I'd had in Madrid but something a lot more intense because I did love Ismael—I just didn't want to talk about my loans, career, or family now because I knew it would be hard for him to understand. Our relationship was going well, and I wanted to avoid talking about the things I was there to forget.

Ismael followed me to the kitchen sink and put his arms around my waist. "Sierra, we can't choose our family. But maybe you should give them a call. You've been here more than a month, and they probably are wondering what you are doing."

"I know. I can't tell them about you, though," I said abruptly and turned to face him.

"I love you, Sierra. It sounds like you have some big problems if you tell me you love me and then can't tell your family about me. I don't want to be your secret. That's not a real relationship."

"My parents are racist. It's not something people

in America go around admitting. If they knew I was dating a poor black guy from Cuba who takes care of orphans and animals, the shit would hit the fan." I paused and looked at his surprised face. I continued, "But you know what? After saying that, it all sounds so absurd that I'm still trying to please everyone. I will tell them. I'm going to call my sister first and tell her right now. This is the new me."

Chapter 34
Face the Music

"Hey Lexie, how are you?" I said over Skype. It was around 3:00 PM in Detroit.

"SIERRA! Oh, my gosh. I was going to call you. We're planning my graduation party for August. You have to come. It is going to be so fun. I just have to pass my summer classes, then come August, I'll be free!" Lexie said, grinning at the camera.

"Awesome, Lex! Way to go! How are you doing with all that?"

"I'm good. How are you? Are you in Madrid, still working at that startup?"

"No, I'm in France."

"Oh my GOD, Sierra! FRANCE?!? What is that like? Are people super rude and mean all the time?"

"Uh, I'm in the south of France in a small city called Narbonne. I'm working at this orphanage animal shelter place, I call it the shorfanage, and, well, I started dating a guy, too."

"WHAT?! Who is he? Is he like one of those super-hot French guys that has long hair and plays soccer?"

"No, he's Cuban, and he's black. And Mom doesn't know, and neither does Dad," I said, like it was a confession.

Lexie stared blankly at the camera for a few

A MINOR DETOUR

seconds. "Is he black or Hispanic?" She sounded confused.

"Yes, he's both, a descendent from Africa. I love him, and I'm going to stay here a while longer. I like it here. The kids are cute, and my life has some purpose for once," I said confidently.

"Oh my God, Sierra. Mom and Dad are going to flip out. When are you going to tell them? I can't believe it. I remember that you wanted to get a good job after business school and to make a lot of money. But instead, you are now working with poor people and dating some Hispanic guy who is also black," she summarized.

"Thanks for being supportive, Lexie. I'll tell them soon or maybe not at all. I am not sure. So, how's Mario?"

"Great! I feel like everything is so amazing in my life. We might move in together after I graduate. He's the perfect boyfriend," she gushed.

"That's really good to hear. I'm going to get going now. Count on me for coming to your party in August. Let me know the details, and please don't tell Mom about my boyfriend. I want to do it on my own, when it's right," I said.

"Don't worry, Sierra. Of course, I will let you know about my party, and it would be awesome if you could make it. I don't know, but maybe try to bring your new boyfriend, too, so we can meet him?

Have a good night." Lexie smiled and then ended the Skype call.

Since my tourist visa expired in April, I was staying illegally in Europe, so I had to leave at some point to go back to the U.S. It wasn't like I didn't want to go home to Detroit, I just didn't want to face the music, my family's tune of how things were supposed to be. I was out of sync with their values.

If I did go back to Detroit in August for Lexie's party, introducing Ismael would not be met with the same approval I had envisioned for Cristian. My parents would want to know what type of job he had before they even met him. And, because Ismael had not gone to college, I could hear my aunt Pattie echo the words to me that she told my cousin when she brought home an Algerian Uber driver: "The Lord wants all of us to be equally yoked, so no one is pulling more than their share. Get it?"

My family was too narrow-minded American for me now. Because Ismael was black and Hispanic, my family also would be confused, just as Lexie was, as to how a black guy could speak Spanish. I imagined my Mom probably would snidely say something like, "My, Sierra, he sure does have some tan," or maybe uncle Ron would chime in with, "Yeah, brother," like he'd done once at a BBQ place after getting too excited over the pork ribs.

I closed out of Skype and checked my email. There was a message from a lawyer with the subject line "Brown and White Lawsuit." I quickly read the short email stating that there was a class-action lawsuit being filed against Brown and White and, if I was interested in learning more, to contact them within the next ninety days.

Realistically, the minor detour to Europe my life had taken the past few months couldn't go on forever. I had more money in the bank, was caught up on my loan payments, and had a boyfriend. This was what I had wanted before I left for Madrid, and how all these things had come together was impossible to explain.

www.ingramcontent.com/pod-product-compliance
Lightning Source LLC
Chambersburg PA
CBHW022019170626
46808CB00003B/984